Diary of a
Young Girl

Diary of a
Young Girl

Mark Anthony

www.urbanbooks.net

Urban Books, LLC
78 East Industry Court
Deer Park, NY 11729

Diary of a Young Girl Copyright © 2010 Mark Anthony

ISBN 13: 978-1-60162-374-4
ISBN 10: 1-60162-374-7

First Mass Market Printing December 2012
First Trade Paperback Printing August 2010
Printed in the United States of America

10 9 8 7 6 5 4 3 2 1

*This is a work of fiction. Any references or similari-
ties to actual events, real people, living or dead, or
to real locales are intended to give the novel a sense
of reality. Any similarity in other names, charac-
ters, places, and incidents is entirely coincidental.*

Distributed by Kensington Publishing Corp.
Submit Wholesale Orders to:
Kensington Publishing Corp.
C/O Penguin Group (USA) Inc.
Attention: Order Processing
405 Murray Hill Parkway
East Rutherford, NJ 07073-2316
Phone: 1-800-526-0275
Fax: 1-800-227-9604

Part I

The Formative Years

Chapter One

New York—1983

Dear Diary,

I was just nine years old when I first held a vibrator. I thought it was a toy until my live-in nanny, Joyce, caught me playing with it and raised her voice, scolding me with her thick Jamaican accent. Unfortunately, Joyce was very sick in the head and on several occasions, either when my dad wasn't home or when she was bold enough to sneak me into her room, she showed me how to use her vibrator. That was just the start of the sexual abuse that I endured at the hands of Joyce. Only I was too young to really know what abuse was. Like I would always feel awkward and instinctively knew that something was wrong about what Joyce did to me, but at the same time I kind of enjoyed it.

See, my daddy was a male whore, never home and always out chasing women so I couldn't run to him. And sadly, my mom had died when I was very young so I couldn't run to her either. Fortunately for me, I loved to write from as early as I could remember. I loved to create stories that were so compelling and believable just so it could help me escape to a fantasy world, a world where I didn't have to cope with abuse or with the reality of growing up without my mom.

Make-believe stories weren't the only things that I wrote about. I also would write about reality in my secret diary. Early on in my diary I would write deep things for my young age. Like I would ask God how come he didn't take some little boy's father away from him, instead of taking my mom away from me. I would write and say that God didn't love Shayla Coleman because if he did, there is no way that he would have taken my mom from me.

I reasoned in my diary that fathers usually help their sons with external things that are outside of a boy's life. Things like learning to tie a necktie, or learning to play baseball, all trivial things like that. But with mothers and daughters it is different, I reasoned. Like only a mom could truly teach her daughter about things that directly impacted her. Internal things. Things like her first period. Training bras for the new bumps that form on a woman's chest. A daughter can trust a mom when a mom talks to her about sex and what is healthy and what is not. A mother can tell a daughter what is a violation of a woman's body. And a daughter can trust her mom to go to her for protection when a violation of her body has occurred, especially if it's a repeated violation.

But, for me, I didn't have my mom physically present to help me. All I had was my diary. It got to the point where I stopped writing about deep things and just started writing about the daily things that were happening in my life. What's funny is before I knew it, those daily things that I was writing about started to take the form and the shape of a full-length novel but I continue to call it a diary. And while my diary may read like a novel, my story wasn't make-believe. My story was real and my story was just that. My story. A story that started with

Joyce "tickling" me with something that was far from a toy and one that progressed into incest, an addiction to pornography, and me living a very promiscuous life.

Chapter Two

The Cycle Continues

My father had an alarm system on our house. It was set up where anytime a door or a window in the house would open a quick, one-time beep or chirp sound would go off, sort of like an alert.

Well, I was almost sure that I heard that beep sound and I panicked like no end.

"Joyce! I think my dad is home!" I blurted out to Joyce in a loud whisper as I jumped up in a panic, trying to figure out just what the hell to do.

"Lawd Jesus!" Joyce screamed in panic and not pleasure as she started scrambling to pick up her clothes.

She screamed at me to take my things and run upstairs as fast as I could. We were in the living room, which was in the front of the house. Thankfully there was a formal dining room and the kitchen that separated us from where my father had entered the house.

"Shayla, go in me room and get dressed! Hurry for ya' fada catch me and kill me!"

I darted toward the stairs and I glanced at Joyce standing in front of the VCR banging on it and yelling at it, trying to get the tape out. This was 1983 and back then VCRs were big and bulky as hell and loud as hell and slow as hell when it came to ejecting tapes.

"Shayla!" my father yelled out to me.

My heart was pounding and I didn't answer him. I just knew that he had heard the porno tape. I was stiff and frozen because from upstairs I couldn't see anything and I couldn't tell if my father had made it into the living room and realized what was going on or what.

"Shayla!" he yelled out again, only this time the yell was louder and filled up the whole house.

I managed to put on my pants and as soon as I slipped them on Joyce came bursting into the room and she locked her door behind her. She was breathing really hard to the point where she was almost hyperventilating. The first thing I noticed was that I didn't see the porno tape in her hand.

"Hurry up and get dressed!" she screamed at me as she hurried and put on her skintight jeans. She almost tripped and fell on her face in the process.

"Shayla!" my father shouted again. Only this time I could tell that he was making his way up the steps.

"Yes, Daddy?" I responded. "I'm in Joyce's room doing my homework," I lied. I didn't know where that lie came from but considering it had been the first day of school, it sounded good and it came off smooth as hell.

"Okay, listen, I got something for you but it's in the basement and I need you to stay upstairs for about five minutes or so until I get everything set up and ready. Okay? Don't come down until I call you."

Wheeeeeewwww. I thought as I blew out some air.

"Okay," I hollered back.

My heart continued to beat a mile a minute but I was so damn relieved at that moment and lucky as hell!

What I later found out was that when my father had initially came home and opened the side door. He had gone directly to the basement so that he could bring in the dog cage, dog food and supplies he was carrying and wanted to surprise me with. That had been the only thing that had prevented him from coming directly into the kitchen and then into the living room where he would have surely caught me and Joyce.

Yup, it was my birthday after all, and my missing-in-action father trying to surprise me was the only thing that had saved my ass from a serious ass whoopin' and Joyce's ass from being deported or killed or sent to jail, or a combination of all of the above.

The reason that my father had told me to wait five minutes before coming downstairs was so that he could go back outside to the car and get the puppy that he had bought for me as a surprise.

Looking back, I don't know if I should thank God for my father not having caught me and Joyce that day or if I should be mad at God for not allowing my father to catch me and Joyce that day.

All I do know is that Joyce and I had dodged a major bullet but the thing was, from that day forward I was hooked on watching "girlie flicks" as Joyce described it, and I was also hooked on touching myself. What was even sicker was that having almost been caught, that sort of provided me with an even bigger thrill, as if I was an exhibitionist or something. What's sad was that I was only in the fifth damn grade at the time and I didn't have a clue as to the seriousness of what I was being exposed to.

Chapter Three

End of an Era—Fall 1986

By the fall of 1986, Joyce had gotten older and somewhat wiser. I never actually knew her real age because on more than two birthdays, Joyce had told me that she was twenty-two. So I knew that she lied when it came to her age. I think that she was always actually seven to ten years older than any age she would ever tell me. She was a pretty woman who reminded me a lot of the actress Jackée Harry who played Sandra on the TV show *227*, only she wasn't as tall.

Joyce had managed to establish herself in this country to the point where she was ready to move on to bigger and better things than being a full-time nanny. She had finally gotten her citizenship and she had also managed to get her associate's degree from Manhattan Community College. With her degree she landed a job at a law firm doing paralegal work. As part of her natural progression she also managed to get herself an apartment of her own out in Queens.

As for me, I had turned thirteen years old and was in the eighth grade. With Joyce having served as my sexual abuser for the past four years I was fast as lightning. I was armed with sexual experience and skills that most married women in their thirties couldn't claim.

I had mixed emotions when I found out that Joyce was leaving. On one hand I was happy for her because she was prospering and progressing. But on the other hand, I was upset because I didn't want Joyce to go. She was like a rock of stability for me in many ways.

With my mom having passed when I was so young, Joyce had been like a mother figure to me. In fact, she was really the only mother figure that I knew. And with my father constantly on the go, chasing skirts and tricking money on chicks, I could never bond with him emotionally the way I desperately had wanted to. So emotionally, I guess it was kind of natural that I latched on to Joyce in the maternal kind of way that I had, regardless of her sick ways.

Joyce had been the one that I had run to when my period came for the first time when I was eleven years old. She'd bought me my training bra and explained to me about cup sizes and all of that. Joyce was the one who had taught me how to cook and how to wash clothes. Joyce taught me about style, fashion, lingerie, and how to walk in heels. She was the one who would wake me up in the mornings to make sure that I was on time for school. She was also the one who would protect me on the few occasions when I'd gotten into altercations with some jealous-ass ghetto chicks from my school in the Canarsie section of Brooklyn.

Yeah, Joyce was definitely like my mom, a big sister, and playmate all wrapped up into one. What was bugged was that by not having my mom around, I had always just assumed that the sexual things that Joyce exposed me to were the things that my real mom would have exposed me to and taught me had she been alive. It wasn't until I got older that I learned differently. In my mind, I thought that all of the girls in my school had a mom who watched "girlie flicks" with them and who tickled them in the same way that they would buy maxi pads for them.

I know it sounds bugged but that was my reality. My reality with Joyce also included the time that she literally stood by and coached me during a threesome. I lost my virginity that day at twelve years old to one of her thirty-year-old jump-offs. Again, I thought all moms were right there in the room with their daughters when they lost their virginity the same way they would be in the room if a doctor was examining their daughter in a hospital or something. How was I supposed to know any different?

Anyway, when Joyce finally left, it sort of marked the end of an era for me. Yeah, Joyce gave me about two hundred and fifty dollars in hush money and she told me that she would stay in touch with me and visit me and check up on me, but part of me just sensed that she was gonna disappear out of my life in the same way that my real mom had disappeared out of my life. And sure enough, after about two months or so had passed I never heard from or saw Joyce again.

My father replaced Joyce with a new live-in nanny named Vera. Vera was cool and she too was a young, pretty West Indian girl but she was definitely no Joyce. Vera was way too uptight and she seemed like she didn't know how to let her hair down. I mean I gave her a chance to see how she would work out but it soon became clear to me that she was not gonna be that mother figure to me that Joyce was.

But it was cool. Joyce had bounced on me and she couldn't be replaced. My pops was still missing in action and I was at the point where I stopped hoping and wishing for his attention.

Looking back, I now know that I had this real big emotional void that I was desperately trying to fill. That is why I probably turned my attention to being desired and noticed by my classmates. I soon got on a quest to become popular and accepted at all costs.

I was only thirteen and in the eighth grade, but I was about to get buck-ass wild!

Chapter Four

Hoochie Momma

I was light-skinned with hazel eyes and naturally straight hair that extended down to my shoulders. I was extremely attractive with an Alicia Keys type of look. At thirteen years old, my five-foot-four-inch body was developed like that of a nineteen-year-old college freshman, complete with big legs, full C-cup breasts, and a nice onion booty. Yet despite all of my physical attributes I never felt like I looked good or was all that pretty.

So despite all of the attention that I would receive from the opposite sex I would always dress in the tightest jeans and the tightest shirts that I could fit into. When it came to shorts, they had to be short shorts. Although I liked wearing sneakers, I preferred to wear heels or some type of sexy open toes shoes or sandals.

To say I dressed provocatively—well, that would be an understatement. A hoochie momma would be a better way to describe how I looked on most days when I would head out of my house and make my way to school.

The thing was that my hoochie momma look did get me the type of attention that I was craving and usually that attention was from guys who were older than myself. For the majority of the time I would get approached by guys who were in high school and in college but more and more I was also the recipient of catcalls and comments from men who looked old enough to be my daddy.

Although I wasn't in high school, my route home from school would take me right past Canarsie High School and put me in constant contact with a lot of the students who went to Canarsie High. That was how I had come to meet this guy who everybody called BK.

BK was a super-senior and he had that sexy, thugged-out look. Me and BK would make small talk every time I would see him. He would always come at me with comments about how good I looked and how I was so sexy and all of that. Usually I would flirt with him as well but I kept it to just flirting. In the back of my mind, I knew that I was eventually gonna call his bluff.

Not much longer after the time that Joyce had totally disappeared on me, I walked into this bodega located on Rockaway Parkway, the same bodega that I would go into everyday after-school. It was at the start of the wintertime so the bodega was sort of like an impromptu after school gathering spot where everyone could gather and escape the cold winds and kick it with each other before heading home.

I walked into the bodega with one of my home-girls named Angie. Angie and I were so much alike when it came to our style of dress and the hoochie momma mentality that it was scary. The only difference between the two of us was that Angie was dark-skinned and I was light-skinned. I mean, I knew that Angie didn't know as much as I knew sexually—in fact, she was still a virgin—but she had this vibe that she would give off and from that vibe, I knew that she would always be open and down for whatever.

Angie and I were both in the bodega just standing around chat-chatting when BK, who was also in the bodega, walked past us. He didn't immediately recognize me, so I playfully pushed him in his back.

"Oh shit! What's up Shayla?"

"How you gonna just walk past me like that and not speak?"

"My bad," BK said while licking his lips like LL Cool J. "With that big ass of yours I don't know how I didn't see you."

I just laughed at BK's comments, but at the same time I loved the fact that he'd taken notice of my ass. I was wearing a Triple F.A.T Goose jacket that stopped right at my waistline. Although it was wintertime and I had to cover myself up to keep warm I made sure that I always showed off my ass no matter what I wore.

"BK, you know you don't know nothing about this," I said while trying to squeeze one of my hands into the back pockets of my jeans while simultaneously placing a blow pop into my mouth using my other hand.

"Angie, you know BK?" I asked.

Angie shook her head no, and I was going to introduce them but BK spoke up.

"I don't know nothing about what?"

"About this," I said as I took my hand out of my jeans and tapped on my ass with my right hand. "You wouldn't know what to do with this!"

I could tell that I had caught BK off guard simply by the way that I had made him blush. Angie began smiling and giggling with embarrassment.

"You hear this chick?" BK asked while tapping his homeboy on the shoulder.

"Don't ask him, because he wouldn't know what to do with this either. Y'all can't handle this," I said and smiled as I sashayed my way out of the bodega, sucking on my blow pop. I instructed Angie to follow right behind me.

"Shayla, you know this dick right here would have yo ass speaking in tongues!" BK bragged while grabbing his crotch.

I didn't respond right away and I began to walk in the direction of East 103rd Street, where my house was located.

"Angie, call me later," I said to her, being that she lived in and was heading in the opposite direction, toward East Ninety-fourth Street.

"You better tell your girl to watch her mouth," BK said to Angie as she went about her business.

"She a big girl, she can handle herself," Angie said, speaking up for me.

As I waited at the light to cross the street, BK yelled out to me, "Shayla, I'm gonna have to come check for you if you keep talking that shit you talking."

I just looked at BK and smiled and then I crossed the street as the light had turned in my favor. For the past two days straight I had been in a horny-ass mood. On that particular day when I was in school my pussy had been jumping and throbbing all day long. I knew that as soon as I got home I was gonna head right to my room and get busy masturbating.

When I was about a block away from the bodega something came over me and it was telling me to call BK's bluff. Another part of me was telling me to just leave BK alone and go home. Unfortunately it was my hoochie side that won out. Without hesitation I turned my fast ass around and walked back in the direction of the bodega. I could see BK still standing around kicking it with his boy.

"BK!" I yelled out to him, but I couldn't get his attention.

"BK!" I shouted out a little louder this time. The traffic had stopped moving as the light turned red so BK was better able to hear me.

"Come here for a minute!" I yelled to him as I gestured with my hand for him to come across the street. I was hoping that his boy didn't come across the street with him, and thankfully he stayed put.

BK walked right up to me. He was wearing the 40 Below Timberland boots and he also had on a Triple F.A.T Goose. He had gold fronts in his mouth and he looked a lot like the rapper Big Daddy Kane, only he was shorter and stockier than Kane.

"What's up?" he asked.

"You tell me?" I said as I put my hand on my hip and began cracking my gum from the blow pop.

BK just looked at me and it took him a moment to catch on. But by his next question I could tell that he knew what vibe I was giving off.

"So what's up with all that shit you was talking a minute ago?" he asked.

"I'm just saying, I don't think you could handle this," I said as part of me was feeling a bit nervous. "I mean, you be talking shit to me everyday, so what's up?"

"What's up?" BK asked as a smile appeared across his face.

"Do I gotta spell it out for you?" I said as I sucked my teeth. "Like I said, you can't handle this." I then began walking away from him. And in my mind I was saying to myself, *I know this nigga ain't scared of my ass.*

"Shayla, I ain't trying to go jail behind no pussy."

I stopped dead in my tracks and I told BK where I lived and that I was a big girl and he didn't have to worry about no bullshit.

"If you as live as everyone says you are then just come to the side door in like a half an hour and ring the bell," I instructed BK while testing his manhood just a little.

BK was definitely starting to look like he was scared and like he was gonna front on me. He had that tough thug look but he was coming across like a straight punk-ass sucker.

"So what's up? You gonna come by or what?"

"You drink?" he asked.

I simply sucked my teeth because I couldn't believe that here I was trying to give this nigga some free pussy and he was straight acting like a bitch.

"BK, if you coming through just come in like a half hour!" I said, raising my voice in frustration before I walked off and headed home.

When I got home I noticed that the house was really quiet and I wondered if Vera was home. I searched the house and I found her in the den watching TV.

"Hey Vera," I said real nonchalantly.

"Hi," she responded, looking really sleepy.

We didn't have the type of relationship where we would sit and kick it with each other so I proceeded to go about my business and I didn't say anything else to Vera. I was contemplating telling her that a friend of mine was getting ready to come over but I decided against it because I didn't want her guard up. If I didn't say anything and just let BK come inside, I felt that I could easily sneak him in and out without Vera even knowing what was what.

After I had been home for about twenty minutes I decided to wait near the side door so that if BK showed up he wouldn't have to ring the bell at all.

I had switched into some white leggings and regular T-shirt and I had on some pink ankle socks with the pom-pom balls on them. I stood by the side door with the main door open and the glass screen door closed. There was a cold draft due to the cold weather. I started to shiver as I waited for BK to arrive. Thankfully I didn't have to wait for too long because BK actually didn't front and he showed up at my side door as we had planned.

"Don't ring the bell!" I said in a whisper as I opened the screen door so BK could see me.

BK had showed up with his same homeboy who was with him at the bodega.

What the hell is he doing here? I wanted to ask but I didn't.

"Go in the basement and just chill for a minute," I instructed BK and his homeboy.

My heart was beating kind of fast because the reality of what I was planning to do had just sunk in. Plus, I had to think about what the hell I was gonna do about BK's boy. Like was I just gonna let him chill in the basement while I snuck BK upstairs? All kinds of thoughts were running through my head, but my first order of business was to try to isolate Vera so that I could sneak BK upstairs to my room.

I headed to the den and I noticed that Vera had actually fallen asleep in the chair that she was sitting in. I got excited because I knew that that was exactly what I needed. As I headed back toward my basement I realized that bringing BK back up to my room might be a mistake. Vera might hear us and wake up. She also might hear the creaking in the floor if we were to go in my room and try to get busy. So my basement proved to be the best spot.

My basement was done up very nice with a bar, a Jacuzzi, wall-to-wall carpet, a nice sectional sofa, and a huge entertainment center. So chilling down there wouldn't be a problem as long as Vera stayed sleep. As I headed back to the basement I was trying to figure out what to do with BK's homeboy. I quickly came to the conclusion that I would have to discreetly tell BK to tell his boy that he had to leave.

"Sorry, y'all," I said to BK and his friend as I made it back to the basement. "I had to lock my dog in the bathroom."

"Here. You drink, right?" BK asked me as he handed me an ice-cold forty-ounce bottle of Olde English malt liquor.

I didn't drink but I decided to just go with the flow and I took a swig of the beer. I hated the taste but I didn't let my facial expression show my disgust. I simply sat down on the sofa and played everything cool. I explained that my housekeeper was upstairs asleep so we had to keep our voices down so she wake.

BK nodded his head to acknowledge my comment. Then he took a real long guzzle from the forty before handing it back to me. His friend had his own forty that he was drinking.

I took another swig from the forty. This time the swig was longer than the first swig that I had taken and it actually didn't taste as bitter as the first swig had tasted.

I rested the bottle on the coffee table that was in front of the sofa that the three of us were sitting on. Before I could blink, BK had pushed up on me. He started kissing on my neck and rubbing his hand on my thighs and before I knew it his hand was underneath my shirt and he was playing with my titties.

My nipples were my most sensitive spot on my body. As soon as BK's hands made contact with my nipples, my pussy started to jump and I could feel my shit getting wet.

BK then tried to kiss me and I kissed him back but in my head I was still thinking about his friend and how it was time for his friend to bounce. Before I could say anything, BK's friend had his hand between my legs and he stated rubbing on my pussy.

"Emmmhh," I moaned as BK kept kissing me. I could taste the alcohol on his tongue and that kind of turned me on and made me kiss him even harder. I wanted to stop kissing him and tell him to tell his friend that it wasn't that type of party but I kept my mouth shut and just went with the flow.

Soon all of my clothes were off and BK and his friend had removed their pants and their jackets but they kept on the shirts that they were wearing. BK and his friend both had nice bodies and they were both packing about the same size.

"I gotta tap this first," BK remarked as he stroked his dick and gently turned me around so that he could enter me from the back.

My pussy was wet as hell and BK slid right in with no problem. I gasped as soon as he slid inside of me because it felt so good. I actually wanted to scream and let myself loose but I knew that Vera was upstairs and the last thing I needed was for her to come downstairs.

BK grabbed hold of a fistful of my hair and he yanked my head backward while he pumped his dick inside of me as hard as he could.

"Yeah, talk that shit now!" BK playfully taunted me as he fucked me. "Can I handle this pussy or what?" he asked me.

I couldn't believe how good BK felt inside of me. Joyce's male friends who I had had sex with in the past didn't feel as good as BK's dick was feeling at that moment.

"Whose pussy is this?" BK asked me as he let go of my hair and slapped me hard on my right butt cheek.

"It's yours!" I replied while still trying to keep my voice down.

BK's friend was still standing next to me stroking his dick but with all of the porno movies that I had seen I knew exactly what to do in a situation like that. I reached out, grabbed hold of his dick, and without asking, I began sucking it as BK continued to fuck me from behind.

About a minute later I was so turned on and I could feel myself about to cum so I began backing my ass up into BK's dick and working my hips until I came. When I came, I couldn't help but moan and gasp. I knew that I was making too much noise because my cocker spaniel that was locked inside the first-floor bathroom started doing this howling bark sound like he was a damn wolf or some shit.

Thirty seconds or so after I came BK pulled out of my pussy and shot his cum all over my back. When he came it was like he had to let the whole world know that he was cumming.

"Shhhh!" I said as I turned and held my finger to my mouth to try and silence BK.

"That's what the fuck I'm talking about!" BK shouted out as loud as hell.

"Mike, come get this pussy," BK said to his homeboy.

What was weird is that his boy was about to fuck me and that was actually the first time that I even knew what the hell his name was.

So Mike came up from behind me and just as he got the tip of his dick inside of me, Vera came down the steps and scared the shit out of me as she started hollering like she'd lost her damn mind.

"Shayla! Oh my God! What the hell are you doing?!" Vera screamed.

"Oh shit," BK and Mike screamed as they scrambled to put on their pants.

"Vera!" I yelled.

"Shayla, get these guys out of this house. Do you know your father will kill you? What the fuck is wrong with you?" Vera continued to vent. She was West Indian but her accent wasn't that thick and for the most part she spoke pretty proper.

BK and Mike had their pants halfway on as they scooped up their boots and coats and fumbled their way up the stairs, tripping over each other and making their way out the door in haphazard fashion.

My heart was beating with fear. I was also embarrassed at the fact that I had been caught. As I scrambled to put on my clothes I also instinctively got mad as hell at Vera because I felt like who the hell was she to be telling me what to do in my house? After all, she was just the fucking maid, for crying out loud.

"Vera, you need to mind your damn business," I yelled as I had gathered my things and began making my way up the steps and out of the basement.

"Your father is gonna kick your little ass. What is wrong with you? Shayla, you're only thirteen years old."

"Vera, mind your damn business," I screamed from the top of the steps as I stormed up to my bedroom.

I knew that my father would kick my ass if Vera told him what had happened, so I grabbed a towel that was laying on my bed and wiped down my entire body. I threw my clothes on and made my way back downstairs. I decided to see if I could reason with Vera in my own irrational way.

"Vera, look. I'm sorry for cursing at you but you don't need to worry about me and there is no reason for you to say anything to my father."

"No reason to say anything to your father? Shayla, you was just having sex on your father's sofa. How do I not say anything to him? You're only thirteen years old. You ain't grown!"

"*Uggghhhh*. Oh my God," I barked. "Vera, I wasn't even doing anything so I don't even know what you're talking about!"

Vera just paused and looked at me like I was crazy and deranged.

"You wasn't doing anything?"

"I mean, so what? I was just kissing a boy and his friend was here with him. Big fucking deal."

"Shayla, you know you was doing more than just kissing. And watch your mouth when you're talking to me."

"Watch my mouth? You ain't my fucking mother."

"You goddamn right I ain't," Vera said in a real patronizing way.

I wanted to just rush her and start whipping her ass but I checked myself. I shook my head and just blew some air out of my lungs. I tried to figure out just what the heck I was gonna do, and more importantly, what the hell was I gonna tell my father?

After all of the times that I had masturbated and watched pornography and used my vibrator and had sex with Joyce either one-on-one or with her different male friends, I had never been caught and I kind of thought that I never would get caught. Unfortunately my number had been called and I had been busted red-handed with a hot dick in my pussy. I just knew that my father was gonna kick my ass when he came home.

After trying to reason with Vera to no avail, I could hear her on the phone dialing my father in an attempt to relay to him what had just transpired.

I was starting to hyperventilate with worry. I realized that there wasn't a damn thing that I could do to change what I had done but right then and there I decided that I was going to straight flat-out deny everything that Vera was gonna claim. Yeah, I was going to make it seem like she was just out to get me and cause a rift between me and my father. I had to put the ball in my father's lap and make him decide who the hell was he gonna believe.

Was he gonna believe his daughter, his only child, his own flesh and blood that he hardly ever was home to see, or was he gonna believe some illegal immigrant maid bitch that he was fucking who barely had a couple of months history with him?

Time was gonna tell.

My father would probably come home to deal with me as soon as Vera made contact with him. I knew that there was nothing that I could do to control that. So I just grabbed my Walkman, put on my headphones, pressed the play button, made my way to my room. I locked the door, plopped down on my bed, listened to Salt-N-Pepa and hoped for the best.

Chapter Five

Do As I Say—Not As I Do

Although it was barely approaching six o'clock in the evening, being that it was wintertime, it was already dark outside. I didn't turn on my television or any lights in my room. Instead, I chose to just lay on my bed in total darkness with a defiant attitude. The volume on my Walkman was turned up as loud as it could go. I turned it up that loud because it was my way of shutting out the rest of the world, allowing me to just lay and chill and be totally by myself.

As loud as the music was I was actually surprised that I'd dozed off. I was even more surprised at what woke me up. When I woke up I couldn't hear a thing other than the music that was coming through the headphones. Yet I literally felt the vibration of my house shaking from what felt like the front door being slammed. It snapped me out of the slumber that I was in. I quickly removed the headphones from my ears, sat up on the bed and nervously listened until I was able to hear my father's voice and confirm that he had indeed just come home.

I could hear Vera talking all animated and out of character and I knew that she was dropping dime on me. Then I heard my father's voice again and after a moment or so I heard complete silence. I prepared for the storm that I knew was about to come up the steps.

I blew air out of my lungs, closed my eyes, put my headphones on, and just waited. Sure enough after about two minutes or so I could hear my father banging on my bedroom door, but I just laid there in the dark with my heart beating fast as hell and I ignored his knocks.

"Shayla, I know you hear me! Now open up this goddamn door!"

Just chill, just chill, I told myself as I tried to relax.

"Shayla!"

I continued to ignore my father.

The next thing I knew the door was violently bursting open from the force of my father's boot kicking it open. Light from the hallway partially filled my room and I could see my father's imposing muscular six-feet-four-inch frame briskly coming at me.

My heart was really pumping now but I didn't move. I stayed stiff with my eyes open and continued to listen to my music.

"Take this shit off!" my father screamed while snatching my Walkman and headphones and flinging them across the room.

"You heard me knocking at the door. Shayla, what is going on with you?" I knew my father's fuse was blown because he had this big-ass vein that would pop out on his forehead whenever he was angry. As he to me it looked as if it was pulsating.

I looked at my father and twisted my lips. I didn't say anything to him.

"A'ight, Shayla," my father said as he held both of his palms faceup in a surrendering gesture. "Okay. I'm gonna try to calm down and talk sensibly."

My father, who looked like he could be related to the rapper Ice Cube, blew some air out of his lungs before speaking again. He asked me to sit up and look at him.

I reluctantly complied.

"Now what the hell is this that Vera is telling me?" my father asked with his face frowned up.

I shrugged my shoulders.

"Shayla, don't give me that bullshit. I asked you a direct question and you better fucking answer me because I'm two seconds from knocking the taste outta your mouth!"

So much for him trying to calm down, I thought to myself.

"I don't know what Vera told you, so how can I answer you?" I said with a neck-twisting Brooklyn attitude.

My father moved closer toward me as if he was gonna hit me and I instinctively braced myself to get hit.

"Shayla, she told me she caught you in the basement fucking not one but *two* niggas!"

I sucked my teeth and shook my head and sighed.

"Shayla, are you crazy or what? You bringing niggas into my house in broad daylight and disrespecting yourself and my house? And what the fuck are you doing having sex? Where did all this come from, Shayla? And forty ounces, what the hell were you thinking?"

I knew that I had to say something and this was as good a time as any to start playing dumb.

"Vera don't know what she talking about," I blurted out.

My father was ready to say something else but I cut him off. "All I did was kiss somebody—that's it. It was a real kiss but that's all I did. So I don't know what Vera is talking about. I knew she was gonna overexaggerate. She gets on my nerves!"

"Vera," my father yelled out for Vera to come upstairs.

Vera had to be at the steps listening or something because she showed up in my room too damn quick.

"I just want you here because Shayla is saying she didn't do nothing but kiss—"

Before my father could finish Vera blurted out, "Kenny"—which was my father's name—"what I told you is the truth. Shayla had no clothes on with her ass up in the air and she was fucking. I know the difference between kissing and sexing," Vera said emphatically as I cut my eyes at her.

Bitch! I wanted to yell at her.

"Kenny, you seen the liquor bottles. There were two bottles because there were two guys in here."

I was getting so heated as I sat there that I wanted to just cry with anger. In my heart of hearts I honestly felt like I did nothing wrong and I definitely wasn't in the mood to be getting chastised.

Before my father could say anything I stood up. I didn't look anyone in the face but I just shouted at the floor. "All right! Y'all want me to say it? Okay, I'll say it! Yes, I had sex downstairs in the basement. I had sex! Your daughter is not a virgin! Big damn deal!" Still angry as hell, I began marching out of the room. But before I could reach my bedroom door my father grabbed me by my hair and yanked me down to the ground and slapped the shit out of me.

"Vera, leave us alone for a minute because I don't want you to see this!"

Whack!

My father smacked me again right across my face. I tried to cover up and protect myself but as a five-feet-three young girl going against a grown-ass man I wasn't having any luck. My father grabbed both of my wrists with just his left hand and with his right hand he repeatedly gave me open-hand slaps to just about every part of my body. He yelled at me the entire time that he slapped earth, wind, and fire outta my ass.

"You're thirteen years old, Shayla! This better be the last time you ever have sex in this house or sex, period! You hear me?"

I frowned up my face and just looked at my father. Although the blows that he was giving me hurt like hell I refused to cry.

"You hear me talking to you?" my father said while smacking me across my face one more time.

"I'm only doing what I hear and see you doing," I shouted.

I could tell that I caught my father off guard because he totally froze for a moment and he had to think about what I just said.

"Shayla, I'm grown and you're a fucking kid."

I was breathing heavy and I still had a look to kill that was plastered across my face. I wanted to say more smart remarks but I kept my mouth shut after that point.

My father stood up straight and he looked down at me while I looked up at him and wondered if my ass-whipping was over.

"Go in the bathroom and clean yourself up and get ready for school tomorrow! And Shayla, you listen to me. You gonna start changing the way you dress around here, and you're gonna start focusing on nothing but your schoolwork. You let this be the last time anything remotely like this happens again! And let me tell you something, you tell those little friends of yours that they lucky it was Vera that caught them and not me because I swear to god I would be going to jail tonight for three murders!"

Are you still yapping? I wanted to ask my father.

I guess he wasn't through because he continued on. "And don't worry about me and what I do and who I do it with! I'm a grown-ass man and I pay the bills around here. I'm the parent and you're the child. You do as I say and not as I do! You understand me?"

I just looked at my father and didn't say a word.

"Now get outta my face because I'm two seconds from killing yo little ass!"

I went and took a shower and nursed the soreness that my father had caused from hitting on me. When I had gotten out of the bathroom my father came up to my room. He talked to me some more and told me how he didn't want to be hitting on me but it was his job and his responsibility to protect me and care for me and that I would shipwreck my life if I got pregnant or some kind of STD. He went on and on and on about all kinds of shit. But when he said that my mother would be so disappointed in me and that she was probably turning over in her grave at that very moment, I almost lost it. I couldn't believe that my father had the nerve to say such a thing.

I tuned him out from that point forward and I couldn't have cared less what he was telling me. *My mother would be so disappointed in me? I* couldn't believe that he'd actually said that to me.

It was all right though, because right then and there I was convinced that I wasn't gonna change a damn thing about myself and I definitely wasn't gonna stop having sex just because of an ass-whipping from my daddy.

In fact, in my mind I knew that I was gonna step things up. Only I knew that I just had to be much smarter about it from that point on. BK's friend Mike had never finished what he'd started with me. As I laid in my bed and tried to go to sleep that night, my last thoughts were me wondering if me and Mike would be able to get it on at *his* house or at BK's house, and if so, when, and for how long?

My pussy was getting really wet just from the thought.

Chapter Six

Kiss and Tell

The next morning when I woke up my father was miraculously home and actually there to eat breakfast with me, something he hadn't done in years. Vera had fixed breakfast and had it on the table yet her black ass was still in the kitchen lingering around trying to busy herself so that she could eavesdrop on what me and my father would talk about.

But I kept my mouth shut the entire time and just listened to my father rant on about how he couldn't sleep at all because he was tossing and turning the entire night thinking about what I had done.

"And when you finish that food go upstairs and change that outfit you got on. I told you last night that you ain't gonna be dressing like that around here anymore!"

"Fine," I said as I used that as my excuse to re-move myself from the table so that I could go to my room and find something other than a tight pair of jeans to put on.

I knew that my father was driving me to school that day so I had to hurry up and change. That wasn't a problem because I desperately wanted to hurry up and get the hell out of that house so I could get to school and be free. In no time I threw on a pair of somewhat loose corduroy pants and a big, thick-ass angora sweater that was not form-fitting.

Fifteen minutes later, after my father had inspected and approved my outfit, we were in his Audi and making the five-minute trek to my school.

"And you make sure that you have those boys' home phone numbers and addresses when you get home from school," my father reminded me for the tenth damn time.

"Daddy, I already told you that they don't go to my school and they're not even from around here," I stressed as we pulled up in front of the school.

"Shayla, listen to me. If I have to drive you to school everyday and go with you from class to class and follow your ass back home, each and every day, well, then that's what I'll do. Now either you get these addresses and telephone numbers so I can talk to these boys' parents or else I'll handle it my way!"

I looked at my father and then looked away and rolled my eyes but I made sure that he couldn't see me.

"All right," I said in a defeated tone. "I'll see you later."

I exited the car, not knowing how the hell I was gonna get out of this jam that I was in, but I knew that I would think of something before the day was out. In fact, I knew that I had to think of something because my father was wild enough and in a position to do just what he said that he would do.

See, my father didn't work a full-time job. Up until the time that my mother had died he used to drive the train for the New York City Transit Authority, but when she died in a car accident he was able to cash in on her million-dollar life insurance policy as well as sue the guy who had crashed into my mom's car. A million dollars may not be a huge sum of money but back in the late eighties if you had that kind of money you were more than straight.

The problem was that my father used the money to just catch up on the years of wild living that he had missed out on because of the fact that he had gotten married to my mother at such a young age. So he didn't move us to some rich, high-class neighborhood out on Long Island. Instead, he kept us right in one of the nicest areas in Brooklyn so that he could have the excess money to finance his nanny jump-offs and his numerous sexual excursions to exotic places like Brazil and Fiji.

So yeah, the last thing I needed was my pops, who had all kinds of time on his hands, literally up in my face following me around 24–7. I knew I would think of something but I just didn't know what. As it turned out as soon as I made it to my homeroom class I found out that I had some much bigger problems to attend to, problems that were much bigger than the problem that my father was posing for me.

"What is that you wearing, girl?" Angie asked me as soon as I sat down in homeroom.

I shook my head and just looked at Angie without saying a word. She immediately knew that I was pissed off about something.

"Are you upset about what I think you're upset about? And why didn't you call me last night? Girl, what's going on? What's up?" Angie asked in rapid-fire mode.

"Just a lot of shit, Angie," I said while still looking pissed off. "And what are you talking about, asking me if I'm upset about what you think I'm upset about?"

"Shayla?" Angie said with this goofy-ass look on her face. "You know."

"I know what?"

Angie smirked and looked at me as if she was trying to figure out just what I was thinking. Then she leaned forward and whispered in my ear.

"Everybody is talking and asking me if it's true that BK and his boy Mike ran a train on you yesterday?"

"What!" I said as I pulled away from her and looked at her in disbelief.

My heart was thumping with shock and nerves.

"Everybody like who?"

Angie sucked her teeth and replied, "*Everybody*!"

I looked at Angie and I still couldn't believe what I was hearing.

"So is it true or what? And you ain't even call me last night and tell me and we supposed to be homegirls? What's up with that?" Angie whispered so that the others in our class wouldn't be all in our business.

"Angie!"

"What?"

"No it ain't true," I lied.

"Well, I don't know. I mean people are talking this early in the morning and word on the street is—"

I cut Angie off. "*You don't know?* Angie, I'm telling you! I'm your girl and I'm telling you what's what!"

There was this pause and Angie and I both looked at each other without saying anything.

The first-period bell rang and we had to make our way to our classes, which were in separate directions.

"Okay, Angie, I'll be straight up with you but you can't say shit to nobody." I paused to see who was around and trying to eavesdrop on our conversation before continuing on.

"I fucked BK yesterday at my house but ain't nobody run no train on me!" I lied in a whisper.

Angie looked at me and smiled a half smile. When her smile disappeared, she spoke up over the loud throng of voices that had filled up the school's hallways.

"Shayla, you my girl and all so don't get me wrong, but all I know is that BK must have kissed and told because people know all your business and all types of details and now you got these girls up in here calling you a ho and all type of shit. So I'm just saying don't get caught off guard by the shit 'cause you gonna hear it."

I needed this like I needed a hole in my head. I was so pissed off at BK that I wanted to slap the shit out of him. But as Angie and I departed and went our separate ways for the time being I realized something that made me feel very stupid. I realized that even if I wanted to get in touch with BK I had no way of doing so unless I happened to just run into him. He didn't go to my school, I didn't know where he lived, and I didn't even have his phone number. I had nothing of the sort, yet I had let him just run up in me and bust a nut on my back like I had known him for years.

Well, there was nothing that I could do all day long but think about what everyone in the school was possibly thinking about me. I wondered who exactly knew what. When did they find out? Did BK just pick up the phone and call everybody last night or what? Did they know that Vera had caught us? My thoughts were driving me insane and there was no way that I could concentrate in any of my classes. I didn't even bother to participate in gym. I just told the gym teacher that I had forgot my shorts and sneakers at home.

The only thing that I wanted to do was hear that final bell ring so I could get home, get on the phone, and start calling around to see who knew what and to also do any damage control.

Before the day could end, though, I had to make it through my lunch period that was right after my gym class at 12:45 in the afternoon. I would always hook up with Angie at lunchtime and she and I would sit together. On this particular day it was no different. The only thing that was out of place was me rushing up to her as soon as she walked through the doors of the cafeteria and bum-rushing her with questions to see had she heard anything more about people calling me a ho.

"Girl, would you calm down and stop bugging out over that," Angie said to me. "No, I ain't hear nothing else about it. And even if I did it ain't none of nobody else's business what the hell you do, so fuck everybody else." She then paused and started to laugh. "I don't mean *fuck everybody else* like go and have sex with them, I mean *fuck them* like don't listen to them. You know what I mean, right?" Angie asked, then she started laughing as if what she had said was the funniest thing in the world.

I giggled with her even though my nerves were shot and I wasn't in no laughing mood.

"You could have at least told me what you was planning on doing yesterday," Angie said to me as we sat down in the lunchroom in our regular spot.

"The thing is it just kind of happened," I said as the lunchroom was quickly filling up with noisy, rambunctious students.

Angie just looked at me and didn't say anything. We were both silent for a little while until she broke the silence.

"So what was it like? How was it?"

"What?"

"You know."

Angie was probing and being nosy but I guess it was normal for her to probe me being that she was my girl. Actually just being around her was helping me to relax and calm me down.

I chuckled and said, "Angie, between me and you, it was so *good*!" I said while emphasizing the word *good*.

I knew that Angie probably wanted to know all of the specific and intimate details but I was smart enough to not be too specific with her because even though she was my girl, I didn't want it to come back later and blow up in my face.

"That's it? It was just good? You know my little hot ass wants specifics, so spill it!"

Angie and I both laughed and just as my nerves had fully subsided, walking past us was this ghetto chick named Sonia who was supposed to be in the ninth grade but had gotten left back so she was still in the eighth grade with me. Sonia was jealous of me because of all of the attention that I would get from the boys and yet even with her trying as hard as hell wasn't nobody ever really giving her ass the time of day. Of course she attributed her lack of male attention to me and I guess I always kept her jealous meter on high.

"*Choo-choo!*" Sonia screamed as she stopped in front of me and looked at me and rolled her eyes. She was with two of her ghetto-ass homegirls and the three of them started laughing.

"*Choo-choo!*" she said again before her and her little crew walked off and went to go sit where they normally sit.

I had a short-ass fuse and a temper that I guess I got from my father. It never took much for me to lose it. Actually I was always surprised that my short fuse hadn't gotten me into more trouble or more fights than the few that it had gotten me into up until that point.

After I realized what Sonia was insinuating, it was like I blacked-out with anger one minute and the next minute I was seeing red. Without saying anything to Angie I left all of my books on the lunchroom table and charged straight at Sonia and snuffed her.

Sonia never saw me coming and neither did her girls. I charged her and tackled her like I was a linebacker trying to sack a quarterback.

She and I both went tumbling into a pile of milk crates that were full of the little school milks.

"Bitch, I'll kick your ass!" I yelled as I grabbed a fistful of Sonia's hair with my left hand and just started repeatedly punching her in the face with my right hand.

"You think you funny, bitch?" I said as I kept punching her. I was laying on top of her chest and relentlessly beating her ass. There were open milk cartons around us and milk was all over my pants and sweater and all over Sonia's clothes as well.

Everything had happened so fast that it took a few moments for everyone to realize what was going on, but when people realized that there was a fight going on, the entire lunchroom went crazy and were gathered around me and Sonia. They jeered and cheered us on like we were two prized pit bulls that were trying to kill each other.

"Don't be swinging on my girl like that!" one of Sonia's homegirls said while simultaneously landing a kick to my ribs. She followed that kick with some punches and before I knew what was what she had grabbed hold of me and pulled me off of Sonia and I was getting jumped.

The only thing that I knew to do was reach out and grab hold of Sonia's hair with both of my hands and I didn't let go of it. I swung her around like a rag doll all the while her friend was still hitting me.

Next thing I knew was that teachers were there separating us and breaking up the fight.

"You fucking ho!" Sonia screamed at me.

"That's why I beat your ass, bitch!" I shouted back while breathing really heavy and being restrained by one of the teachers.

I glanced and saw Angie. I asked her to grab my stuff for me and to keep it in her locker until I saw her again.

The entire lunchroom was buzzing as announcements were repeatedly made for everyone to go back to their seats.

Sonia, myself, and her friend were all carted off to the dean's office. While we made our way to the dean's office I felt nothing but elation as I looked at Sonia's face and saw the bruises and the scratches that had been inflicted by yours truly.

I knew that I was probably gonna get suspended from school but I can honestly say that I didn't care. Getting suspended would probably be a blessing in disguise because it would distract my father's attention from wanting BK and Mike's personal information. The rumors about me being a ho would also have a chance to die too, especially since I had kicked Sonia's ass. A good ass-kicking always made for better gossip than rumored sex. So I felt good about what had just transpired.

Chapter Seven

Drastic Actions—Drastic Measures

My father was called by the school and briefed on the lunchroom brawl that I had. He was informed that I was gonna be suspended for a week and that he had to come to the school and pick me up and escort me home. Needless to say, when he arrived at the school he had a look to kill.

Thankfully he didn't act ghetto and start cursing at me or trying to hit me. What pissed me off was that when he saw me he didn't immediately ask me what had happened. Instead he immediately confronted the dean and introduced himself and apologized for my actions.

What the hell you apologizing for? I wanted to blurt out but I kept my mean mugging look on my face and didn't say a word.

My father then asked the dean if the two of them could talk in private for a moment, so they stepped out of his office and into the hallway. They had closed the door behind themselves so I couldn't hear what they were talking about, but to be honest I really didn't care. I was still in fight mode and my temper hadn't yet totally subsided even though it had been nearly an hour or so since the fight had ended.

"Again, Mr. Blakely, I want to apologize for my daughter's behavior. I can assure you that nothing like this will happen again," my father said as he and the dean, Mr. Blakely, had come back inside the office.

"Like I said, Mr. Coleman, Shayla is a wonderful student. I am sure that this is an incident that will not escalate, but due to the policies and procedures of the school system, unfortunately suspension is the disciplinary action that we must take."

"No, no, it's understood. Shayla, you owe Mr. Blakely an apology for the way in which you acted and disrupted his day and disrupted things in general."

Are you for real? I wanted to ask my father.

But what was the use in resisting at that point? "I apologize," I solemnly said to Mr. Blakely without making any eye contact with him.

My father and I made our way out of the school and into his car and we headed home.

My father still had this look to kill and I was still heated and wanted to bring it to Sonia some more. As we drove home I was actually shocked that my father literally didn't say a word to me the entire time. Occasionally I could feel him staring at me but I refused to return any looks in his direction. Instead, I just slumped in my seat and thought about the fight and what I could have done better. I was pissed off that Sonia's homegirl had managed to rock me with the few shots that she had caught me with, but it was all good because I knew that if she fought me straight up I would whip her ass.

Well, the ride home wasn't too long because we didn't live that far from the school. As we pulled into our driveway my father told me that he didn't want me leaving the house for any reason for the next week. He also told me to go up to my room and to just leave him the hell alone because he had a lot of shit to think about and that he was so pissed off with me that he couldn't stand to look at my face.

That was fine with me because it wasn't like I was in no talkative mood anyway. So what if I couldn't leave the house for a week? As long as I had my vibrator I knew that I would be good. In fact, I would be in heaven. A whole week of no school, no homework, no studying, and literally nothing to do but chill and do what the fuck I wanted to do? I was cool with that.

So I made it to my room and sat on my bed for a moment. In the back of my mind I was still kind of pissed off at my father for not having even asked me anything about Sonia or what had sparked the fight and for not taking my side. He had pretty much taken the side of the school and the girls that I had been fighting, yet it had always been him who had told me to never take shit from anybody and that if somebody was bullying me or anything like that then I should stand up to them or else risk being a daily target of that bully.

As I thought about that I realized that I had to confront my father on it because he was contradicting himself. I got up from the bed and I marched right down to the kitchen where I saw my father and Vera sitting at the kitchen table talking. In fact, I had overheard my father saying something in reference to my aunt but I hadn't fully heard just what he was saying.

I walked into the kitchen and headed straight for the refrigerator. I played it off like I had come to get a drink.

"Shayla, didn't I tell you to go to your room? I ain't ready to look at you yet!"

"Can't I get something to drink?" I asked with exaggerated drama and disbelief.

My father looked at me and told me to hurry up and get the drink and to get out of his sight.

As I poured myself some orange juice I spoke up and said, "Daddy, honestly I don't think I need to be punished for this. You saying you don't want me to leave the house but that's not fair because you're the one that always told me to stick up for myself and don't let people disrespect me and bully me and that's exactly what I did. And now you're mad." I said what I said and I walked out of the kitchen. I was trying my hardest to use reverse psychology on my dad.

"Shayla, I don't wanna hear that bullshit! Just stay up in your room until your aunt gets here. She's on her way."

"Whatever," I said under my breath and made my way back up to my room.

My father had no sisters so I knew that he was referring to my mother's sister Tanisha. I loved my Aunt Tanisha because she was so cool. She always took me to places like Coney Island, Great Adventure, Disney World, and all that family vacation stuff. Since I didn't have any brothers and sisters, it was like her kids were my brothers and sisters because we were around the same age and we basically grew up together; during summer vacations and major family holidays and weddings we would always be together.

Aunt Tanisha had gotten divorced and then remarried and although she still lived in Queens, not too far from where we were currently living in Brooklyn, I hadn't seen much of her or my cousins ever since her wedding to her new husband. Her new husband had three kids—all boys—from a previous marriage, so with Aunt Tanisha's three kids—all girls—from her previous marriage, their house was like a modern-day black *Brady Bunch,* minus the maid. I knew that Aunt Tanisha had her hands full with her new family so I didn't take it personal when I started to see less and less of her.

A part of me did dread the fact that she was getting ready to come over to the house. I dreaded it because I knew that my father was gonna fill her in on all of the drama that had taken place during the past twenty-four hours.

Sure enough, when Aunt Tanisha arrived, my father called me downstairs and summoned me to sit at the table in the dining room where my aunt was sitting and waiting.

My aunt was a gorgeous lady. She was in her early forties but she looked so good for her age. She looked like a voluptuous Halle Berry. And you always smelled my aunt before you saw her. I say that because her perfume, while it always smelled good, was always so intoxicating and filled up any room that she was in. And that day was no different. Aunt Tanisha stood up from the table and she walked toward me with her sexy high heel leather boots and tight boot-cut jeans.

"Oh my god, look at you! I can't believe how thick you getting, looking *just like* Lisa when she was your age." Lisa was my mother's name. "Come give your auntie some sugar."

I loved whenever someone mentioned me and my mother in the same breath when it was in a positive light. I cracked a huge smile and I gave Aunt Tanisha a nice warm hug. What was weird was just like that, in an instant all of that anger and hostility that I had been holding onto since the fight, it just evaporated into thin air.

"Tanisha, you want something to eat or drink?" my father asked.

Tanisha declined, saying that she was good.

"Well, Shayla, I want you to know that I filled your aunt in on what has been going on with you over the past couple of days, and the truth is, Shayla, I have to admit that I'm kind of scared for you. It's like I think I know why you're do-ing what you're doing and it's because of your mother. With your mom not here for you you're acting out, trying to get that love and attention that only a mother can give to you."

I looked at my father and didn't say anything. I was slipping back into pissed-off mode because I didn't need him or want him to be telling Aunt Tanisha all of my business.

"Shayla, no matter what I do for you or provide for you, I can't replace your mom. I just can't. I'm a man and I will think like a man, react like a man, and reason from a man's point of view. I think I might be doing more harm for you than good."

I nodded my head and looked at my father as if to say hurry up and get to the point.

"Shayla, do you know what next Monday is?" my aunt asked.

I thought about it for a minute and I paused without saying anything. But there was no way I could front like I didn't know.

"Yeah," I quietly said.

I knew that it was the eighth anniversary of my mother's death.

My aunt looked at my dad, and then she spoke up.

"Baby, I can be wrong, and your father could be wrong, and if we are then please forgive us. But your father told me about what happened yesterday and then the fight you had today at school. I just want you to know that I still love you, your father loves you to no end, and because we love you we have to look out for you and do things that are in your best interest, especially when we see you doing things that are dangerous and not good for you."

I nodded my head as I looked at my aunt. I respected her way too much to even remotely disrespect her. She was talking to me as we sat at that dining room table like she always spoke to me, with respect and compassion and not casting all type of judgment on me.

"What I think, Shayla, is that without you really realizing it, you're looking for your mother's love—not sex, like you had yesterday. Your anger today when you had that fight in school is just your lashing out at not being able to be loved the way you want to be loved by your mom. I could be wrong, Shayla, but I don't think I am, and I don't think it's a coincidence that these things are happening right around this time of the year when your mom passed." Aunt Tanisha looked at me with this look that said she really wasn't trying to offend me and that she really meant well.

I turned my lips slightly and I blew out some air. A part of me wanted to believe what my aunt was telling me, but in the back of my mind it just seemed to me that the only reason I had sex with BK and his friend was because I was horny! The reason that I had the fight in school was because

Sonia had tried to disrespect me. It was that plain and simple. But I didn't say anything, I just went with the flow. Because had I said anything about me just being horny, or me fighting because I had been disrespected, I felt like I would have also had to talk about my vibrator, and the other times I had had sex. All of that wouldn't have made any sense to my aunt and especially not to my dad. If there was one thing that I was not going to do, that was tell on myself.

"So Shayla, what your aunt and I think is best is if you go and live with her for a while and see—"

I cut my father off. "Go live with Aunt Tanisha?" I asked with all kinds of confusion.

Are you serious? I wanted to ask my father. *Now you're abandoning me too?* I thought.

"But Daddy, I'm sorry about yesterday and today! I am! I mean, okay, I know I was wrong and acted way out of line and all of that. But I don't wanna have to leave because of that. It's not fair."

My father and my aunt looked at each other and my father spoke up.

"Shayla, look, you are too young to understand just how drastic and dangerous it is for you to be having sex—unprotected sex at that—and drinking liquor, and going to school and fighting, but it *is very* drastic for those things to have happened and to have played themselves out the way they did. As your father, it is my responsibility to take care of you and protect you, and drastic actions require drastic measures. What I and your aunt feel is best is if you go and live with her for a while. You don't know it yet but it's gonna help you tremendously."

I looked at my father like I wanted to murder him. I shook my head because I felt in my heart that he had just used what I had done as an excuse to ship me off, not for my benefit like he was claiming, but for his own selfish benefit. With me out of the picture he would be able to come and go as he pleased without having even the slightest sense of guilt when it came to wondering how his actions would affect me.

Chapter Eight

A Queens Thing

Aunt Tanisha then spoke up and she also tried to explain why she also thought it would be good for me to move in with her.

"For how long? I mean, are you just shipping me off until I'm grown?" I rudely asked my father. I directed everything toward him and not toward my aunt because I knew that he had simply manipulated her into going along with his plan.

"Shayla, I'm not shipping you off! That's the first thing. And as far as how long, I think it should be for as long as it takes for you to bond with your aunt and your cousins and get that negative energy out of your life."

Negative energy? I wanted to ask my father just what in the hell was he talking about. He was trying to use sophisticated terms and shit to confuse me and I could see right through that. But instead I kept my mouth closed and just nodded my head and listened.

If there was one thing about me, it was that I was a fighter. I also had an unbelievable will. As I sat there with my aunt and my dad, my fight mode kicked in and so did my strong will. I decided right then and there that if my father was gonna ship me off because of what I had done during the past twenty-four hours, then that was cool. That was the decision that he had come to and I would have to live with it for now.

I wasn't gonna beg him to let me stay or beg him to rethink what he had decided. Nope, I wasn't gonna cry and I wasn't gonna break. I was gonna go with his wishes and do what I had to do. I also knew that I wasn't gonna cause my aunt any trouble but at the same time I was not gonna change who I was for nobody.

I was still gonna dress the way I wanted to dress, I was still gonna screw who I wanted to screw, and I was still gonna stand up for myself whenever anybody disrespected me. My father's slick power move of wanting to ship me off had opened my eyes. It taught me that from there on out I could still be me. I could still get buck-ass wild but I would just have to be smart as hell about it.

As I looked back and thought about those twenty-four hours that had triggered the decision to move me to Queens, I realized that my mistake wasn't that I had fucked BK and Mike, rather it was that I had been sloppy about the whole thing. That sloppiness led me to getting caught and it led to BK and Mike opening up their mouths. That was what led to me beating Sonia's ass and ultimately that was what led to me getting shipped off by my dad. It was like one bit of sloppiness on my part had started an avalanche of events.

Cool. I was ready to take those L's on the chin and keep it moving. I learned from what I did wrong and I was determined to do me and be me at all costs even if my father wanted to disown me!

Fuck him, I thought.

I was ready to move to Queens and do me.

Chapter Nine

The Power of the Pussy

It was now 1987 and I had been at my aunt's house for a minute. My aunt lived in a nice middle-class section of Queens that is known as Rosedale. Rosedale, which is a predominately black neighborhood, had many two-family houses where one family would live on the first floor of the house and another family would live on the second floor. Each floor had its own entrance and its own bathrooms, bedrooms, kitchen, living rooms, and dining rooms, so there was more than enough space for each family.

With the size of my aunt's new blended family, what her and her husband Pete decided to do was purchase a two-family house they converted that to function as a one-family house. It was smart the way they did it because this way it was spacious and with all of the people in the house it never really felt overcrowded or cramped. In fact, there were six bedrooms in total and with my oldest male cousin, Earl sleeping in the comfortable finished basement, everybody had their own bedroom.

Well, in the beginning of my stay at Aunt Tanisha's everything was cool. For the most part things continued to be cool but the newness of my presence and the novelty of me moving in with my cousins was just about wearing off. That was especially so for my female cousin Leah, who I was forced to share a room with.

Leah was a year older than me and she was a sophomore at Jamaica High School. Based on our age we had a lot in common and in the beginning we clicked. Leah liked boys and she liked many of the same things that I liked. She wasn't nearly as fast and as wild as I was but I couldn't fault her for that.

Being that Leah and I had to share her full-sized bed and share her room in general, I guess she started to feel that I was invading her space and cramping her style somewhat. It soon got to the point where her whole vibe and demeanor became cold and distant when it came to her interacting and dealing with me.

It was wild because you would have thought she had a split personality or something. One day we were cool and she was talking to me and letting me wear some of her clothes and then it was like out of nowhere she was barely speaking to me. She stopped letting me wear her clothes and then all she started to do was complain to both me and her mom about how *Shayla sleeps so wild, Shayla won't make up the bed, Shayla keeps my room messy, Shayla is always on the phone,* and on and on. It just wouldn't stop.

But I was cool about it and I was also smart about it. Not once did I ever get confrontational with her. I just sucked it up, dealt with it. I always apologized to her and my aunt and promised to do better at whatever her issue was with me.

In my mind I was starting to see a pattern—or at least I thought it was a pattern—and that was that people would always find a way to abandon me or become distant toward me. I could never understand it. Now Leah was becoming distant toward me and abandoning me. Before her it was my pops. Before that it was Joyce, and before Joyce it was my mom who had abandoned me. Sandwiched in between all of those people, BK had also distanced himself from me and abandoned me. But with BK it was more like he had dissed me big-time.

In fact, after that day in which he had fucked me in my basement, he literally never spoke to me again. If I would see him somewhere in the street or at the mall or wherever, he wouldn't even acknowledge me except for telling me things like "bitch get the fuck outta my face." Real insulting shit like that. It was like he had hit it and quit it. To me that probably hurt just as bad as my mom leaving me because I really thought that me and BK could bond and be cool even if it was on just a sexual level. I guess I was wrong and I realized that it must have been something about me that turned people off.

Back to my cousin Leah, she was at that point where she was turned off by my presence. Believe me, the last thing I wanted to do was be around somebody that didn't want to be around me.

Maybe God was looking out for me or something because just as Leah and I started to go south with our relationship, my relationship with my cousin Earl started to click. Earl was nineteen years old and he was enrolled at a local college called York College. I don't know if it's because males click better with females or what but I soon found myself constantly in Earl's presence.

In fact, Earl's basement apartment-like setup soon became my new oasis. I started spending most of my time down in the basement just kicking it with him and his friends, playing video games, watching movies, or just bugging out.

Even though I was young and inexperienced in a lot of aspects of life, there was something that I knew I had a natural gift for and that was when it came to picking up the type of vibe that a person was giving off or trying to send out. Like with me, for example, I always gave off this loose, free-spirited vibe. I guess you could call it a whore vibe. Being that I gave off that vibe I almost always recognized that vibe when others would be giving it off as well.

Well, with Earl he definitely gave off a whore vibe as if sex was always on his mind, as if he would be down for whatever, whenever, and wherever.

One day, right around the start of the spring in 1987, Earl, myself, and two of his homeboys from York College were in the basement watching a tape of Eddie Murphy's *Delirious*. While we were watching the tape I noticed that Earl, who was sitting next to me on the sofasofa, kept putting his hand on my thigh and moving it as if he were massaging it. He wasn't moving it toward my crotch; he would move his hand toward my knee area. He was doing it really subtle, which to me is what made it seem sensual and which is also why it was turning me on.

He did this throughout the movie but I didn't say anything and I didn't ask him to move his hand. I simply went along with what he was doing because I needed to confirm the vibes that he had been sending off to me. This was the best kind of confirmation that I could get.

My plan wasn't to stay quiet for too long, though, and when there was about fifteen minutes or so left of Eddie Murphy's performance I nonchalantly titled my head back toward Earl's head, which he had reclining on the headrest of the sofa. I whispered in his ear very quiet and discretely, "you better be careful touching me like that."

After I said that I smiled slightly and then just kept watching the tape. I could tell that Earl looked at me but he didn't say anything. When he didn't move his hand from my leg I could tell he had caught on to what I had said in the manner in which I wanted him to catch on.

It was a Friday night, around 8:30 or 9:00 P.M., so after the movie ended, Earl and his friends were trying to figure out just what they were gonna get into for the night. As they sat around discussing their options, one of Earl's friends opened up a bottle of Bacardi that he had.

"Nigga, you was sitting here all that time with that shit and you ain't tell nobody!" Earl said to his friend Rory.

"Cheap-ass nigga! Give me that shit."

Earl took the bottle and cracked it open . He went to his refrigerator and took out two cans of Pepsi. He poured some Pepsi and Bacardi into four glasses, one for each of us, and he put some ice cubes inside each of the drinks.

I was somewhat apprehensive about drinking because of my experience with beer and its bad taste, but I didn't want to seem like I wasn't down and then have that be the reason for Earl abandoning me and becoming distant with me. I couldn't risk that so I drank the Bacardi and Pepsi. To my complete shock, it actually tasted good! I mean, it was like all I tasted was the soda.

Thinking that Earl probably didn't pour that much liquor in my glass because he was testing me or something, I quickly downed my drink and asked Earl for some more.

"Goddamn, shorty! You throwing them shits back like a quarterback," Rory blurted out.

Earl didn't say anything as he complied with my request and poured me another drink.

"Earl, you trying to get your cousin fucked-up or what?" his other friend asked.

"Nah, she a big girl, she can handle it," Earl said to me as he looked at me. I knew exactly what he was insinuating.

"Yeah, I can handle it," I replied with a smile and I gulped down some more of my drink. Once again as I drank I noticed that all I could taste was soda. I loved the fact that I didn't taste that nasty-ass, bitter taste that beer left me with.

In no time I was buzzing from the liquor and feeling nice as hell and I became extra talkative.

"So y'all just gonna go out and get into something without me?" I asked.

Earl and his three friends looked at each other and they smiled.

"Oh, okay, y'all dissing me! That's cool," I replied and I was feeling so good that I just went and turned on the radio, tuning the dial to Mr. Magic's rap attack radio show.

"Nah, it ain't that. It's just that you ain't ready to hang out where we hang out," Rory replied.

I was now buzzing like crazy from the liquor and I started dancing to one of the Biz Markie songs that was playing. I think it was the song "Nobody Beats the Biz."

As I danced I unbuttoned three of the buttons on my blouse and revealed some of my cleavage.

"I might be young but I got the body to get me over," I replied as I kept on dancing.

"Yo, she is fucked-up!" Rory replied. "Don't give her ass no more liquor."

Earl, Rory, and their friend all started laughing as I walked up to Rory and started grinding my ass on his crotch.

"You think I'm fucked-up?" I asked him with a smile. "Let me hang out with y'all tonight and I'll prove you wrong."

Rory didn't dance with me; he just smiled and nodded his head to the music but I knew that I was making a good impression on all of them.

Then Earl spoke up and said that he was just gonna chill in the crib for a minute to make sure that I didn't throw up or do anything crazy to alert my aunt that I had been drinking. He told Rory and his other buddy to head to Rory's house and that he would call over there in a few minutes to hook up with them later.

"Shayla, take it easy."

"Yeah, it was nice meeting you," Rory and his other friend said to me as they made it out of the basement and went about their way.

I had never been drunk before but I also knew that I had never felt the way I was feeling at that particular time so I assumed that I was drunk.

"Shayla, you one crazy girl," Earl said to me as he put the dirty glasses in the kitchen sink.

There was this funny part in the *Delirious* tape that we had just been watching where Eddie Murphy is imitating Ralph Kramden and Ed

Norton from the TV show *The Honeymooners*. In Ralph Kramden's voice Eddie Murphy imitates Ralph saying to Norton, *"Hey Norton, hey Norton, how would YOU like to fuck ME up the ass?"*

Something clicked in my head and I just started laughing uncontrollably when I thought about that part of the tape. I was also laughing because of the liquor. I was laughing so hard that I could barely speak as I imitated Eddie Murphy talking like he was Ralph Kramden. I repeated the joke and I fell out on to the sofa in laughter.

"Yo, Shayla, you are tore-up for real," Earl said.

"No, I'm not. I'm good, I'm good."

"You gotta maintain when you go back upstairs. I don't want Tanisha cursing my ass out," Earl remarked.

I paid his remark no mind because I felt giddy and drunk but I also felt fine at the same time.

"Hey Earl," I shouted out with a grin on my face, trying to hold back my laughter.

"What's up?" he asked.

"How would YOU like to fuck ME?" I said in a tone that mocked Ralph Kramden's voice while pointing my index finger at Earl and then pointing it back at myself. After I'd said that I burst out into laughter.

Earl began cheesing from ear to ear. He shook his head and said, "Yo, Shayla, you are really bugging right now!"

Although I was drunk, I remembered to keep my golden rule about still being buck wild but just being smart about it. The liquor combined with Earl's vibe had my ass horny as shit but I knew I had to be smart.

I wanted Earl to know that I wasn't bugging and that I was serious. So I walked right up to him and stood on my tippy-toes and started tongue kissing him. Sure enough, just as I had suspected, Earl went with the flow. In fact, he started kissing me back. He was kissing me hard and passionate as hell like he had been storing the kiss up inside of him.

The next thing I knew my tits were exposed and Earl was sucking on my nipples.

"Come in here," I said as I grabbed Earl by the hand and led him into his own bedroom, which was just a few feet away from where we had been standing. Keeping to my rule of being smart, I made sure that he had a lock on his door and that it was locked.

With the door to his bedroom locked I felt more at ease and I quickly disrobed. Earl didn't speak a word to me and he also started taking his clothes off. His dick was hard enough to cut diamonds.

"You happy to see me?" I asked as I resumed kissing him.

"I wanted to fuck you since you got here," Earl said to me as he pulled away from me. He pushed me back onto his bed and started eating me out.

"Why didn't you?" I asked as I simultaneously moaned from the pleasure of his tongue.

"Because you my cousin," he said as he came up for air.

His tongue was feeling too damn good so I decided to shut the hell up so that he wouldn't stop sucking on my clit.

As Earl sucked and licked my clit I realized that on paper we were cousins but technically we weren't cousins because he wasn't Aunt Tanisha's biological child. Truthfully though, even if he was Aunt Tanisha's biological child I would have still wanted him and we would have just been kissing cousins for real.

I grabbed onto Earl's head and I squeezed it as hard as I could because I was cumming. I couldn't believe how fast that I came but I guess it was from the alcohol or something. I don't know but I was cumming and it felt good as shit.

"Was that shit good?" Earl asked me.

"Em-hmmhh," I replied as chills ran down my body.

Earl flipped me over onto my stomach. He entered me from the back and began stroking away. I was as wet as a river and his dick felt so good inside of me that in a matter of like twenty strokes I was hollering into his pillow and cumming for the second time.

My pussy must have felt good to Earl because right after I came he pulled out of me and he came all over his bedsheets before plopping his body down on the bed next to mine.

We both then laid there on the bed breathing really heavy and not saying anything to each other. From out of nowhere the thought of how BK had played me and stopped speaking to me after we'd had sex entered my mind.

That fear was quickly dispelled as Earl became the first guy to hug me or kiss me after sexing me.

We cuddled butt naked on his bed and he told me that he was happy that I'd come to live with them.

"Really?" I asked

"Word."

"I'm glad I came too," I said. Then I laughed as I realized the play on words with the double reference to the word *came.*

"What's so funny?" he asked.

"Inside joke," I replied.

Earl and I stayed there in each other's arms for about ten more minutes. I knew that I was pressing my luck in terms of possibly getting caught, so I got up and started to get dressed.

"What's up with round two?" Earl asked as I slipped on my panties.

"Round two?" I said with a smile.

Earl just looked at me.

"Tomorrow," I said. Even though I wanted to get it on and poppin' again right then and there I remembered my rule.

"A'ight, just make sure you keep your promise," Earl said as he got up from the bed.

We soon were both dressed and ready to open the door and leave Earl's room. Although the buzz from the liquor was fading, I was still feeling like I was floating on cloud nine and on top of the world. It was at that moment that I remembered the unspoken lessons that I had learned from Joyce, especially when it came to getting money for sex without even asking for it. What it taught me was that there was this inherent power when it came to sex, especially taboo sex. Although I didn't want any money from Earl he had something else that I wanted and I knew that right then was as good a time as any to make my move.

"Earl, is this a sofa bed?"

Earl looked at me and replied that it was.

Being straight up, I told him what I was sensing from Leah. I asked him would he mind if I asked Aunt Tanisha to let me move into the basement with him and sleep on the sofa bed as my permanent bed.

Earl paused and thought about it.

"We could have as many rounds as we want to if I was sleeping down here," I said to Earl with my puppy-dog eyes while making sure that I was mustering up the softest voice that I could.

Just like Joyce would give me the money and the McDonald's back in the day to keep my mouth shut, I knew that in the back of Earl's mind he would also want me to keep my mouth shut, so I had a good feeling that he would go along with my plan.

"Yo, I'll be with it but we just have to agree on some shit first," Earl said.

"Okay, like what?"

"You can't be running your mouth about the shit that I do. Like I smoke weed, and I don't want that shit getting back to nobody. Or if I have a shorty down here, I don't want you being rude and shit. You know what I'm saying."

I knew exactly where Earl was coming from and he didn't have to worry about me dropping a dime on his ass because if there was one thing I wasn't, it was a snitch.

"Earl, if there is one thing you don't have to worry about with me it's me being a snitch or pissing you off over something silly. Snitches get stitches is what they say back in Brooklyn."

Earl laughed and said that he liked that slogan.

"Well, then it looks like we need to have one more drink to toast to us being roommates," Earl said as he headed toward the kitchen to get some glasses.

Yes! I screamed inside my head.

That's the power of the pussy! I thought as I laughed to myself.

Chapter Ten

Ain't No Party Like an Underground Party

A week or so after Earl and I had sex, I approached my aunt about the move to the basement. Surprisingly she was cool with it and agreed to it without giving me or Earl any kind of resistance. I was actually surprised that Aunt Tanisha didn't say no or say something like she would have to check with my father to see what he thought about it. Not that my father would have given a shit, but I just looked at it as being something that she would at least want to run by my dad. However, my cousin Leah was beefing and complaining about something each and every day. I think it was that pressure that had forced my aunt's hand and allowed her to give in to my request.

It took all of about two days for me to realize that I was gonna absolutely love living in the basement with Earl. I had finally escaped Leah's her bitchy stank-ass attitude and escaped to Earl and his cool, carefree way of living. It was bugged because in a lot of ways Earl's free-spirited, anything-goes attitude reminded me a lot of my old nanny Joyce.

Like Joyce, Earl was into pornography and he had a collection of porno movies and porno magazines that dwarfed Joyce's little collection of three videotapes and two magazines. Similar to how Joyce had different guys coming to see her when my father was not around, Earl also had different chicks who would stop by to see him or call him.

The thing I think I liked about Earl more than Joyce was that Earl was more into what the latest trends were. He was way cooler than Joyce. Maybe it was because his age was closer to mine or because he was a guy and I was a girl, I don't know, but I do know that I could relate really well to Earl and we clicked right from the start.

Earl introduced me to weed and taught me how to roll a joint and how to inhale the shit without killing myself. He also introduced me to liquor. He taught me about the different brands and types of liquors and what mixed best with what, or as he would put it, he showed me the difference between *girlie* drinks like strawberry daiquiris, and *manly* drinks like Hennessy on the rocks.

With Earl being young and his hormones racing, he became the best sex teacher that I ever had. I mean, Joyce was good and she taught me a lot about how to please my own body, but Earl taught me a lot about how to please a guy's body.

Unless Earl had gone out, or was chilling with one of his shorties, or was with his homeys, literally every night he and I would end up watching porno movies and fucking each other. I loved every moment of it.

Earl taught me the proper way to suck dick and deep-throat dick so that I would drive a man crazy. With Earl I was able to practice and do a lot of the sexual positions and freakiness that I would see on the porno tapes. For instance, I would let Earl ejaculate in my mouth because it was something that I had seen all of the porno girls do I wanted to experience it and with Earl I was able to. With Earl I was able to experience anal sex for the first time. The shit hurt like hell and I didn't enjoy it, but with Earl being the good mentor that he was, he was able to get me to relax during anal sex and not be so tense. Soon enough, with the right lubrication I had become an anal sex queen and I actually started to enjoy it.

Throughout the whole time that Earl and I had our little hedonism thing going on in the basement, I remembered my rule of remaining buck wild but being smart as hell about it. I definitely didn't wanna mess up the good thing that I had going with Earl and get shipped back upstairs to room with one of my female cousins or worse, get shipped back to live with my dad. The move to Aunt Tanisha's had worked out way better than I'd ever imagined or thought it would. Therefore I made sure that I had knocked out my schoolwork and did my part around the house, such as washing dishes and shit like that, without having to be told to do it.

Sure enough, by the time the summer rolled around I had my aunt, and my dad for that matter, eating out of my hand. They were overjoyed and adamant about how they were so right that coming to live with Auntie Tanisha was the best thing that could have happened to me. They even eagerly agreed with my wish to attend high school in Queens.

I was no dummy. Wanting to keep my sex thing and free-living thing going, I played it up like a professional con artist.

As I would say to my aunt and my dad and my uncle, "Yeah, at first I didn't think I would like it here, but I was so wrong. I feel like I have three sisters now and three brothers. I love it because I was never this close with anybody in my family before."

My aunt, my uncle, and my dad would soak up all of that type of talk. And think that they were social geniuses and that they had helped to boost my self-esteem. Little did they know that all they had really helped to do was feed the demons that were inside of me that Joyce had planted some years ago.

Like I said, Earl was better for me than Joyce had been because he was hip to all of the latest shit in the street and he would teach me and keep me up on everything. That was never more true than when Earl hipped me to these underground parties that him and his boys would go to. From the way he described the parties I was dripping with anticipation to the point where I felt like life itself couldn't continue on until I had gone to one of these parties that Earl spoke so fondly of.

"Nah, Shayla, you ain't ready for this shit. Plus, I wouldn't feel right introducing a girl to something like that. I mean, guys can go up in those type of spots and it ain't nothing 'cause that's what we do. But with chicks, it's different," he reasoned with me as we spoke about him taking me to an underground party with him.

"Different like how?"

"It's just different."

Earl paused and we both didn't say anything.

"Okay, put it like this. If I was a chick I wouldn't wanna be up in spots like that," Earl stated as he sat on the sofa in his basement and I sat on one of the bar stools.

"Why not? Just explain it to me," I said, sounding kind of frustrated.

"Because niggas will start looking at you like you a ho or some shit. Just like you was telling me about how you had to get in that chick Sonia's ass that time when she was basically trying to call you out as a ho, you'll be dealing with that kind of shit all the time if word gets out that you be up in these parties."

"Earl, here's the thing, I know where you coming from but I'm just saying, all I wanna do is go check it out. That's it! Besides, I'm from Brooklyn, I'm not from Queens so don't nobody out here know me. Plus, I'm gonna be going to school out here in Queens so it's not like I'll even be seeing the same people that I saw last school year. I won't know anybody and won't nobody know me out here so if they talk about me won't nobody know me who would even give a shit," I reasoned.

"Let me think about it."

"Earl, think about what?" I snapped back. That was the one thing that I didn't like about him. At times he could act like a real bitch-ass nigga. I was used to Brooklyn niggas like BK who never came across with no bitch-ass shit. They was always straight up like real street niggas, but then again Earl wasn't a street nigga.

Earl could sense my frustration with him. He finally relented and agreed that in two weeks he would take me to one of the underground parties. He reasoned that I needed to get off to a good start at school. It would help keep my aunt's guard down and she would give me the okay to go.

I went along with Earl's reasoning but I wondered just what was it that he was really trying to keep me from. See, the way Earl described these underground parties it was more like underground sex parties. People would organize through word of mouth and meet up at different locations that would constantly change. At these locations, which were usually somebody's house, there would be strippers and hoes there along with guys looking to fuck.

According to Earl, usually the strippers would perform and after they performed they would give private dances or go off into private rooms and fuck any willing and paying customer. Since

I loved sex as much as I did, the whole idea of a sex party just fascinated my young ass. I looked at it as being no different than if I loved basketball and couldn't get enough of it and then somebody comes to me and tells me about this basketball league where other players from all over the city come to play in an organized fashion. Why wouldn't I wanna join a league like that? In the same way why wouldn't I wanna go to an underground sex party even if I was just gonna be a spectator?

Well, that was it.

Earl and I had set the date for two weeks after school started and I couldn't wait to go. In the interim I had started attending Thomas Edison High School in Jamaica, Queens. The school was cool. It was located literally right across the street from Jamaica High School and within walking distance from another high school called Hillcrest High School. I knew right away with all of those schools in such close proximity that I was going to like going to school in Queens a whole lot better than school in Brooklyn, simply because with so many people I would be able to blend in better and do my thing without worrying about developing any kind of bad reputation.

At Thomas Edison I continued to dress the way I had been dressing when I was going to school in Brooklyn. I noticed Thomas Edison was that there were a lot more better-looking girls than me and there were a lot more chicks who dressed better than me. I knew that eventually as time went on I would have to figure out a way to steal the attention away from the other chicks and put it on myself, but that would come later. The more pressing issue at hand for me was just focusing on my schoolwork so that I could stay off of Aunt Tanisha's radar and get to this party with Earl without any hitches.

Thankfully, the two weeks came and went. I was now only fourteen years old, a freshman in high school and about to attend my first underground sex party.

Being that the party was taking place on a Saturday night, Earl convinced my aunt to allow me to go with him and his friends to the last showing at this movie theater in Valley Stream, Long Island called Sunrise Cinemas. We had managed to leave the house around eight in the evening. We told my aunt that we would first be going to the mall to hang out and then we would be going to the last show that was scheduled to start just before eleven that night.

My aunt didn't object and she trusted Earl to do the right thing by me, and again, it was because I was being the model niece in her eyes.

Of course, as soon as Earl and I left the crib we headed in the opposite direction of the movie theater and instead we headed over to pick up his boy Rory. We made our way to the sex party in my uncle's Nissan Maxima as Earl drove and sipped on some Hennessy.

By this time I had become an expert at rolling weed. That was what I did in the front seat as Rory drank from a Heineken bottle.

"Yo, where this shit at?" Rory asked Earl over the loud music.

"Over at this crib in South Side off of Sutphin Boulevard," Earl replied as he added that there was supposed to be a bunch of Puerto Rican chicks coming there from the Bronx.

I reclined in my seat and smoked the weed that Earl had given me. I couldn't help but feel inadequate with the way that I was dressed. Other than my tight jeans I looked way too regular and I could only could imagine how out of place I would look. I decided to not stress and see what was what when we got there.

When we finally made it to the crib we parked the car and Rory walked over to a tree to piss out some of the beer that he had been drinking. When he was done we made our way to the side door of an old, shabby-looking two-story house.

Earl knocked on the door and we were greeted by a big linebacker-looking bouncer. Apparently he recognized Earl and nodded that it was okay for us to enter. As we entered Earl paid for me and him to get in—I think it was like ten dollars apiece—and Rory paid his way in. After paying the entrance fee we were then patted down and frisked by another bouncer before finally being let in.

Once in we made our way to this dimly-lit living room where there were a bunch of guys standing around but there were a whole lot more half-naked chicks in stilettos who were walking around.

We were on the first floor but from upstairs on the second floor I could hear loud music being played.

"What's up y'all?" a thick, dark-skinned black chick in a slingshot thong bikini and clear stilettos asked me, Rory, and Earl.

"They with you?" she asked me.

"It's not like that," Earl replied.

"Y'all wanna dance?" she asked as she pushed up on Earl in a seductive manner. "Ten dollars for a wall dance and twenty-five for a private dance," she added.

Earl sized her up and the next thing I knew was that he was telling me to just chill right there and that he would be right back and then he disappeared with the girl.

"That nigga don't waste no time," Rory yelled into my ear as by now the music was turned up and it sounded like we were inside of a club or some shit.

"Where did he go?" I yelled back into Rory's ear.

"Prolly off to get his dick sucked," Rory responded real nonchalantly.

Damn! I thought to myself. I mean, I was a fast-ass freak but I didn't know it was like that. I mean, the chick just walked up to Earl and in less than two minutes she was off to suck his dick? That was crazy even for me. But the thing was I realized that she was getting money and after thinking about that I knew that I couldn't knock her hustle.

"Yo, I'm about to go get a private lap dance from one of these shorties up in here. You gonna be a'ight?" Rory asked me.

I looked around and the place looked real seedy but I figured that I would be cool, so I nodded my head.

"Okay, but listen, they don't like people just standing around and not spending money and shit so go to the kitchen and get a drink or something. They got a bar and drinks around that way," Rory said to me as I tried to figure out how in the hell did he know that.

So I made my way to the kitchen, which was right next to the bathroom and the kitchen was packed with people. There were dudes everywhere just standing around drinking and flirting with chicks. But I also saw a chick sucking a nigga's dick just straight out in the middle of the kitchen as the dude leaned up against the wall. And to the left of them was some other chick getting fucked doggystyle by some dude.

Where in the hell am I at? I had to ask myself. I mean, I liked what I saw but at the same time I had never seen nothing like this before so it kind of bugged me out and scared me just a bit, but it was more of a nervous rookie kind of scared.

I managed to make my way to the liquor and I began helping myself to a drink. "I got that for you, miss," a guy in a black shirt said to me.

"It's five dollars a drink. What you drinking?" he asked.

"Hennessy and Coke," I said as I reached into my tight-ass jeans for some money to pay the dude with.

"Drinks ain't free?" I asked, sounding all new and shit.

"Free?" the guy asked as he looked at me like I was weird while taking my money.

I didn't respond and I guess my lack of response had thrown him off.

"Oh, you working? Yeah, well then, drinks is free for you. Pardon me, love. My bad, I mean I just ain't never seen you before," he said while handing me my money back. "You can get changed right in that bathroom right over there."

"Ohh shit!" some other dude said, who looked like he could be old enough to be my father. "This some nice tender roni shit right here," he said as he grabbed my ass. He reeked of alcohol.

I looked at him but I didn't know how to react.

"Let me get first dibs at you after you change, a'ight sweet young thang!" the guy said to me as he handed me a fifty-dollar bill.

"I wanna love you PYT, pretty young thang! I need some lovin' PYT pretty young thang and I'll take your there," the old drunk dude sang to me. He sang loud enough for everyone in the kitchen to hear him as he slurred the words to the Michael Jackson hit song.

I looked at him and smiled but I was smiling more so because I was shocked and embarrassed more than anything else.

"Emhhh-uh! Look at that shit right there! Look like a nice spring chicken," the old pervert said as I walked away from him. He apparently thought that I was making my way to the bathroom to go get changed where the other chicks were getting changed at.

That wasn't my destination as I somehow snaked my way through the throngs of people and made it back to the living room. And when I got there I saw that there were four chicks dancing and performing a lesbian show on each other and they had the guys going crazy and throwing all kinds of money at them.

As I watched them I noticed that I was getting extremely turned on and I guzzled down my drink and bopped my head to the music.

"What's up, lady?" a guy said to me as he came up from behind me and grabbed my waist while simultaneously stuffing money into the front of my pants.

"I'm chillin'," I said as I played things cool. The liquor that I was drinking, combined with the weed that I had been smoking earlier, helped to loosen me up.

I reached and grabbed the money that the guy had stuffed in my pants and I noticed that it was twenty dollars.

"So what's up?" the guy asked me.

I finished drinking my drink and I turned to look at the guy and I noticed that he was cute as hell. He was a light-skinned pretty boy with good hair.

"Whatchu wanna do?" I asked.

"That was my down payment, I wanna buy that right there," he said as he came close to me and grabbed me on my ass. "I ain't never seen you at one of these parties before."

At that point I got a bit nervous because I knew what the guy wanted but I was still kind of scared.

"This my first time at this spot," I said while I tried to relax.

"Oh, word?" the guy said as he licked his lips.

I didn't say anything and I knelt down a bit to put my drink down on the floor since I was finished with it.

"So let's go upstairs," the guy said as he handed me eighty more dollars. He put the money in my hand and kind of guided me toward the stairs.

Shayla you are straight buggin'! I screamed at myself.

But unfortunately, the little bit of saneness that I had left, it lost out to my insanity as the guy took me into one of the four bedrooms that were located on the second floor.

"Go into that room right there," some big black guy sitting on a folding chair in the hallway said to me and the light-skinned pretty boy.

We went into the room and closed the door. There was one single bed in the room and a roll of paper towels and a lamp. That's it. There was nothing on the walls and there was no carpet on the floors, no chairs or nothing. I was actually surprised that there was even a sheet on the bed.

The light-skinned dude didn't waste no time. I guess he could tell that I was new so he kind of led me. He turned on the lamp that dimly lit the room and then he started to unbutton his pants.

"Take them shits off," he instructed me as he pulled at the button to my jeans.

It was like I was in a trance and I couldn't believe that I was gonna let myself do what I was about to do. But like a robotic dummy I started to unbuckle my tight pants and I squirmed my way out of them somehow. And I was soon standing there with my socks on and my top still on along with the light jacket that I was wearing, but my ass was fully exposed and just blowing in the wind.

The guy had to have had one of the biggest dicks that I had ever seen and he began to stroke it in order to prepare it for action.

In my mind I was like, *okay, should I kiss the nigga? Should I go down on him or what?* I didn't know what to do so I decided to just turn around so that my ass was facing the guy and

I placed my hands on the bed and just sort of waited for him to fuck me.

"Damn shorty, you ain't got no condoms?" the guy asked.

When he said that he almost snapped me out of my trance as I realized just how crazy I was. But before I could react the guy knelt down and reached in his pants pocket and got a condom and he put it on.

He then knelt down and hocked and spit in my pussy to lubricate it and he slipped his dick inside of me and started fucking me harder than I had ever been fucked in my life. He was so big and handling me so rough that I couldn't help but scream. Although he was being rough and he was hurting me, at the same time the shit felt good and I think just because of the fact that I was sexing some complete stranger, that too was turning me on and before I knew it the guy had me cumming all over his dick and me screaming at him to fuck me harder.

Even with the loud music that was being played I could tell that the guy heard me because he pumped his dick harder and harder into me as he commented on how nice and tight my pussy felt.

Then it seemed like before I could blink it was over, but it was actually more like five minutes or so had passed and I could tell that the guy was cumming as he stayed inside of me and pushed me on top of the bed and pumped his dick until he had completely finished.

"Yo that shit was good, shorty!" the guy said as he lay on top of me breathing real heavy. "*Whewwww!*"

As the guy prepared to get up I couldn't believe how good he had made me feel and at the same time I couldn't believe how extra wet my pussy felt.

"Oh, shit!" the guy screamed out.

"What happened?" I said but as I looked I quickly realized that he didn't have to answer me because I saw him standing there with a rock-hard ten-inch dick that had a ripped condom around it.

"The fucking condom broke!"

I jumped up and my heart started racing a mile a minute. And the funny thing is that I was more scared about getting pregnant than I was about getting some kind of STD. The only thing that I could think of is if I got pregnant how my aunt would be so disappointed in me and how my father would surely whip my ass.

I looked down at my pussy and thick white semen was just oozing out of it. I immediately grabbed the roll of paper towels and I started wiping my pussy clean as if it was gonna prevent any possible damage at that point.

The guy meanwhile had started to put on his clothes and as he got dressed he cursed me like it was my fault.

"Bitch, what the fuck is wrong with you! I can't believe this shit!" he said as he stormed out of the room in somewhat of a panic.

I was definitely rattled as I rushed and put my panties on and I managed to quickly squirm back into my jeans and prepared to head back downstairs.

"Yo!" the black guy sitting on the chair in the hallway yelled at me as I placed one foot on the top step.

"Thirty dollars! You think you live here or some shit? These rooms ain't fucking free!" he said to me.

I was now really rattled as I gave the guy thirty dollars and headed back downstairs to the living room.

I saw Rory and Earl and they were high as hell and enjoying the lesbian show that was still going on and which had been joined by more women.

Over the loud music I yelled into Earl's ear, "Earl, let me get the key. I wanna sit outside in the car."

"Yo, where was you at?" Earl yelled back.

"I went to go get a drink."

"Are you crazy!" Earl yelled. "Niggas will slip some shit in your drink up in here! Yo, stay by me, we gonna be outta here in a minute."

I didn't let up and I insisted that Earl give me the key so that I could go back to the car. My nerves were shot and I needed to smoke some weed in the worst way.

As Earl handed me the key and I turned to leave, here came that old-ass perverted-looking man who had given me the fifty dollars. Truth be told, he wasn't that old. He looked like he could be about in his late thirties or early forties but there was just something sick and perverted-looking about the dude who also looked like he was torn down and beyond drunk from liquor.

"Oh, there go my young tender roniiii, my *fiiiine* sprrring chicken, my PYT come give me some Pussaaay," he yelled out in a slurred drawl over the music. "You tried to disappear on me?"

Earl turned to the guy and told him that I was his sister and that he had to back the fuck up off me.

Then the guy started getting belligerent and started cursing and calling me outta my name and saying all kinds of disrespectful drunk shit.

"I paid that ho *fiffffty* dollars and I want my dick sucked!" the guy said as he slurred his words. "Bitch, come suck this dick!"

"What?" Earl responded with an attitude as he looked at me for confirmation.

I played it off like I didn't know what the guy was talking about and that he was just some wino drunk nigga.

"Yo, go to the car, Shayla!" Earl commanded me.

I quickly left and went outside as Rory and Earl handled the drunk dude.

I got in the car and turned on the radio and realized that it was approaching eleven o'clock and that the so-called movie that we were supposedly going to was just about ready to start.

Like a drug addict I frantically searched that car for the weed that Earl had stashed and when I found it, it was like I had hit the jackpot or something. I quickly rolled a joint and started smoking it. And when it was done I rolled another one and started smoking that one as if I was chain-smoking cigarettes.

But soon enough my nerves calmed down and I was mellowed out from the weed and I reclined in the seat and repeatedly told myself not to worry and that there was no way in the world that I could be pregnant.

Just relax, Shayala, you'll be fine, I told myself.

I blew out some air and I listened to Kiss FM. I realized that there was no way I could tell Earl—or anybody, for that matter—exactly what I had allowed myself to do that night. Yeah, I knew that I would have to suck it up and just deal with it on my own. And at that point I wasn't sure what I felt about underground sex parties. I mean, the open sex and anything-goes type of atmosphere definitely sat well with me. But for the first time in my life, after all of my promiscuity, I was actually scared as hell for the position that I had put myself in. So in that respect I didn't like the danger that underground sex parties had posed for me. But if there was one thing that I knew, it was that even in spite of my fear of the dangers that underground sex parties posed, there still was never a party that I'd been to in my life like the underground party that I had just left.

Yeah, I was scared and confused and excited all at the same time.

Don't worry about nothing I told myself as I lay in my bed that night after finally reaching back home with Earl.

Okay, I'ma chill, relax, and not worry, I said as I stared at the ceiling in my aunt's basement. I had just finished sexing Earl about half an hour earlier. I guess he had gotten all worked up at the underground spot and when he came home he knew that he had a sexual outlet in yours truly. It was all good, though, because the raw dick down that I got from Earl definitely helped to put me at ease where I could in fact just chill, relax, and not worry. Part of me, though, did really hope that I hadn't caught anything from that dude at the party because I would have hated to have passed anything on to Earl. Earl was a good dude as far as I was concerned.

Anyway, I pulled the covers up and over my head and turned on my side into the fetal position, which was my most comfortable sleeping position. And as I closed my eyes for the final time that night just before I fell asleep my last thought was, *ain't no party like a underground party.*

Chapter Eleven

Ho Drama

I had never told Earl about what really went down with me at the first sex party in terms of how I had ended up sexing that complete stranger, or how I had accepted the fifty dollars from that older dude and never gave him anything in return, nor did I feel I had to tell Earl about that.

What was weird was that before Earl had ever taken me to one of those underground parties, he had been real hesitant and almost resistant to take me. He never verbally said it but I just felt like he really cared about me and had a soft spot somewhere for me and he didn't want to corrupt me and expose me to such a crazy, underground world. But as it turned out I was actually wrong about Earl and he quickly proved to be a self-centered, selfish motherfucker and his front to not wanna expose me to that underground world had been just that, a front.

Like I said before, Earl wasn't a street dude. He was down and he was cool, and he was hip to what was going on in the streets but he wasn't a thug, not even remotely close to a being a thug. I mean, he was in college, for crying out loud, and not too many real thugs are in college. But I guess his college smarts, combined with his savvy, was what had planted the idea in his head that he could start pimpin' me at those underground parties.

As open as I was to sex and trying new things, I was pretty much down with anything. So Earl got kind of slick and eased his pimp idea on me as he reminded me how at the first party that I could of gotten myself hurt if someone had slipped a mickey into my drink.

"Yeah, niggas be slipping shit in a bitch's drink and the next thing you know is you wake up the next day in some hotel room or some basement somewhere groggy as hell and not even realizing that like ten dudes then ran all up in you the night before."

I nodded my head and took a shot of tequila as I listened to Earl speak.

"See, what I wanna do is start taking you with me to these spots every week. I mean, it will be just like the spot that we went to in South Side but I want you to see what different spots are like."

I smiled and I told Earl that I was with that, just as long as he could creatively get me out of the house so that Aunt Tanisha wouldn't start bitching about anything.

"Let me worry about Tanisha," Earl said. Being that Aunt Tanisha wasn't his biological mother, he always called her by just her first name.

"I'll be able to get you to go but I want you to be able to enjoy it more when you go. Like last time you had that old dude harassing you and all of that. That shouldn't have went down and the reason that it did is because I wasn't clear at the door with everybody that you was with me. So from now on all I gotta do is pay the tip in to get you in and let niggas know that you rocking with me and everything will be all good."

I took another shot of tequila and told Earl again that I was with it just as long as he could get me out of the house.

"And what will happen is if niggas wanna holla at you I'll be right there with you and they can pay me so that you don't got to worry about collecting money and all of that. You can just go do your thing and have a good time. Or if you wanna drink you can just tell me and I'll get it for you. You think you can be down with that?"

"Of course," I said to Earl, not realizing how naive I was being and just what exactly what I was agreeing to.

See, the thing was, I had realized something after that first night at the first sex party that I had gone to. And that was that the pattern that Joyce introduced me to—the pattern of sex for money—and it was still in full effect. Like that first night, for example, I had grossed 150 dollars in no time and walked away with 120 dollars and I didn't really have to do much for it.

So with Earl asking me to start going with him on a regular basis, I was definitely with it because I knew that I was gonna be making money doing something that I would do for free and something that I liked doing, which was having sex. And with the money, I knew that I would be able to stay up on the latest gear without having to ask my father or my aunt to take me shopping. I mean, my father had the money, and my Aunt Tanisha's husband owned a successful publishing company so even with her it wasn't like taking me shopping would have been an issue. It was just that I wanted to be able to do for myself. And I guess that do-for-myself mentality was always in the back of my head because in the back of my head I always felt like I would end up being abandoned by everybody, so I never wanted to be too dependent on anybody for anything as far as I could help it.

So sure enough, two weeks after Earl told me that he would start taking me with him to the sex parties, he followed through on his promise. He even bought me some real provocative shorts and tight T-shirts and clear high heels that he had me change into when we reached the sex party.

Maybe it was my tight, youthful body, or it was my ass that was hanging out of the shorts, but as soon as I had changed into the outfit that Earl had bought for me, guys were attracted to me like bees attracted to honey.

Thankfully, I did have Earl there to play gate-keeper for me and he regulated all of the different guys that I either fucked, gave blow jobs to, or gave lap dances to.

Thing was, I enjoyed every minute of the attention. I also enjoyed the sex but I have to admit that some of the derelict-looking guys I didn't enjoy too much, and I had to put up some kind of boundaries, so with those types of dudes I would only get twenty dollars from them for giving lap dances; I wouldn't go any farther with them.

After my first night I was hyped like hell because I had actually gone through the entire process and being that the party took place all the way up in the Bronx, I felt good about not having to be labeled a ho by anybody that I knew because I didn't know anybody from the Bronx. I was also hyped because I knew that I had made like 600 dollars that first night with Earl serving as my gatekeeper, or so I thought.

The next day, though, Earl ended up only giving me 100 dollars and I flipped!

"Earl, stop fucking playing with me and give me my money!"

"Yo, you gotta understand that I got shit that I gotta pay and shit that I'm taking care of!" Earl responded. He tried to holler back at the same level that I was hollering but he kept his voice down out of fear of alerting my Aunt Tanisha, who was upstairs in the kitchen at the time.

"Earl, for real, stop playing with me," I barked.

"Shayla, I bought your shit for you to wear and I'm the one that introduced you to the shit and you saying that I can't take my cut?"

"Earl, stop playing stupid. I made over six hundred dollars and that cheap-ass shit you bought me from off of Jamaica Avenue you know it ain't cost you more than fifty dollars. So how is your cut like five hundred dollars and mines is only a hundred?"

Earl looked at me and twisted his lips and just basically ignored me and walked away and went into his room and closed the door. He dissed me basically. And when he did that that same rage that I had when I beat Sonia's ass that day in the lunchroom, it returned and my temper kicked in.

One thing about me that I hate is that when my temper kicks in I don't give a shit about anything or anybody and I completely just lose it. And that is exactly what happened when I saw Earl close his door on me like that.

I charged the door and didn't even bother to turn the doorknob. Instead I just kicked it open.

"Earl, I'm not fucking stupid. Give me my money," I screamed at him.

"Bitch, is you crazy?"

"I ain't no bitch, now give me my money, Earl!"

"Yeah, you ain't a bitch! *Ho,* is you crazy?" he said as he slapped me and grabbed me and threw me on the bed.

"Keep your fucking voice down before Tanisha comes down here," Earl screamed at me.

"Don't be hitting me and I ain't no ho!" I screamed at him. I felt like being called a ho was the worst thing that anybody could do or say to me and that just intensified my anger and I got up off the bed and went straight at Earl and threw a right-hand punch at his face. The punch didn't land flush on his face but the ring that I was wearing managed to graze Earl on his cheek and it cut him clean across his face.

"Ah shit!" Earl winced in pain as he grabbed his cheek.

I kept throwing blows at him as fast as I could and I hoped that all of them were landing, but I couldn't tell for sure because my eyes were closed. And I guess it was a good thing that my eyes were closed because about ten seconds later I felt something knock me upside my head and I went straight to the ground and all I heard was this ringing sound coming from my ears and my head was stinging.

"What the fuck is wrong with you?" Earl screamed as I tried to regain my senses. His one blow had literally walloped my ass and knocked me senseless.

"Look at my face," he said as he grabbed me by my hair and tried to get me to look at him. I tried to look at him but I was seeing double and I couldn't focus on his face.

"You see this blood?" Earl screamed.

He then mushed my head to the ground and I heard him rumbling around in his room. He then came back over to me and he punched me in my face and kicked me in my stomach. I grimaced and winced and cried out in pain as I gasped for air since the wind had been knocked outta me.

"Shut the hell up!" he barked as he stuffed something in my mouth and then held it in place by tying something around my head. It felt like a T-shirt.

I wanted to fight back but I felt like I had just been in a fight with a heavyweight boxer and lost. So I didn't have the ability or the strength to fight back even if I wanted to.

"You wanna scratch mothcrfuckas, swing on motherfuckas, and bark on motherfuckas?" Earl screamed.

Then he went to his door and closed it and locked it and he came back to me and grabbed both of my arms and held them behind my back and he began tying them with what felt like a silk shirt or some other silky material. I tried to wiggle my arms free and as soon as I showed the slightest resistance Earl whacked me upside the head with his fist.

He finally had my wrists tied behind my back and then he ripped off my pants and my under-wear. He pushed me to where my face and my chest were facedown and laying on the bed and my knees were bent and resting on the floor and now that my pants and underwear had been ripped I was there in his room half–passed out from the blows he had given me and with my bare ass exposed.

"So you ain't a bitch, right?" Earl asked me in a gritty, devil-like tone. "Yeah, I know you ain't, but you are a fucking ho," he said as he answered his own question that he'd asked me.

After he'd said that I felt him ramming his finger inside of me and I grimaced and tried to scream but with my mouth closed shut my screams weren't doing much.

Then I felt Earl forcing himself inside of me and it hurt like hell because I wasn't ready for that.

Again, I let out what I thought was a loud scream but it was so muffled that it had to be going on deaf ears.

"Matter fact, you my fucking ho," he said as he kept jamming me with his dick. It felt like he was ripping my insides apart.

I was scared as hell but I was still mad as hell and at that point I decided to stop screaming because I didn't want to give him the satisfaction of knowing that he was dominating me.

"Yeah, look at you, you stopped screaming and you enjoying this shit now. Right?" Earl asked me.

I didn't answer.

"I said right?" Earl screamed at me as he re-grabbed a fistful of my hair and pulled it and twisted my head and neck in the process. I swear I thought he had broken my neck.

Just to stop the pain I nodded my head to show that I was in agreement with him.

He then pushed my head back down on to the bed and resumed raping me.

It was definitely my worst sexual experience ever!

Thank God, Earl soon pulled his dick out of me and for added humiliation he ejaculated right into my eyes and he laughed throughout his moans of ecstasy.

When he had completely finished he smacked me across my face. Not hard. In fact, it was just a tap. And he repeatedly tapped me in my face like five or six times just to humiliate me.

Then he grabbed my face and pressed his fingers deep into my jaw and my cheeks and he forced me to look at him, but I couldn't because his semen was burning my eyes.

"We gotta get something straight," he said to me as he spoke directly into my face.

"Number one. You don't ever say shit about this to *nobody!*"

He then paused and it was like he was waiting for a response from me. And after I nodded my head to show him that I understood him, he continued on.

"Number two. You my damn ho now and you gonna keep coming with me to make this money! You understand that?" he yelled as he pushed my face into the bed.

Again I nodded my head and just hoped that Earl would untie my arms.

"Now just lay there for a minute," Earl barked at me as he walked out of the room and from the sound of it he had gone into another room in the basement where he always stashed his weed.

While he was out of the room I realized how powerless I felt and I was pissed off to the point where I started crying. But his semen was still burning my eyes and when I cried it made it worse, so right then and there I sucked it up because I knew that I had no other choice but to just suck it up.

I knew that I was indeed powerless and with my father not really giving a shit about me, I knew that I didn't have too many options in terms of places to go and at that point in my life, Earl's basement was the best option for me as far as where I would live.

So even though Earl wasn't this powerful, controlling street nigga I knew that I still had no choice but to be his ho. Yeah, I was gonna suck it up and take that major L that Earl had just dished out to me and I was gonna endure what I had to endure.

But right then and there as I kneeled against the bed with my arms tied behind my back and with cum in my eyes, I also decided that I had to come up with a plan so that I would never, ever be dependent on anybody. I realized that it was always my dependence on other people that put me in the positions that I found myself in.

Yeah, I would be Earl's ho. But I was gonna be a ho with a plan.

Chapter Twelve

Heaven to Hell

One of the weirdest feelings in the world that I had to endure was interacting with Earl in the days that followed him raping me.

It had taken several hours for the headache to disappear after he had knocked me upside my head, and it took several days for the burning sensation in my vagina to go away. But emotionally I knew that it would take me much longer to get over the powerlessness and the violation and humiliation that the rape had caused me to feel.

As much as I wanted to be cool with Earl and talk to him like everything was everything, I just couldn't. All of my interactions with him from that day forward were terse and guarded. In fact, I even became that way with people in my school. It was like overnight the rape had caused me to become real distant with everyone.

The basement living space that I shared with Earl and that I had once viewed as this heaven-on-earth oasis now felt like it was a tomb trapped in hell with Earl serving as the devil.

In my heart, I could feel that Earl felt bad for how he had violated me but his pride and arrogance wouldn't let him even bring up the fact that he had raped me, much less apologize to me for it. Instead, he would try his hardest to spark conversations with me or offer me drinks and weed or try to get me to chill and watch a movie with him. I would do it, but my heart wouldn't be in it. Since I was his readily accessible supply of pussy, he still tried to push up on me and kiss me and feel all over me and fuck me on a daily basis. What's wild is that I believe my aunt kind of knew that something wasn't right and I think she knew exactly what was up, but I believe she was just in "protect Earl at all costs" mode. Probably the best way for her to protect him was to act completely ignorant and clueless to shit and not ask any questions or watch things with a suspicious eye.

I'll probably never fully understand why, but even after the rape, whenever Earl would push up on me in a sexual way, I would not resist him. I would always let him have his way with me. Unlike before, I was now only allowing him to sex me for physical reasons, so I could feel close to someone, cum and numb that human pain that I was feeling. Emotionally I felt absolutely nothing at all from the sex. It was like I was on sexual autopilot or something. What I think is that instinctively I just went on autopilot so that I could continue to be accepted by Earl even if it was him accepting me just on a disrespectful level.

What was also wild was that my fight for Earl's continued acceptance was also one of the things that made me continue to go to the sex parties with him and get pimped by him. For me that was only *one* of the reasons why I continued to go to those parties. The other reason was because I knew that I had to start developing a list of *paying* sex clients to help support me for what I was planning on doing.

See, I looked at it like this: I'd fallen in love with the newfound freedom that I was exposed to when I initially started living in the basement with Earl. After tasting that freedom I knew that I didn't wanna give it up, but at the same time things had become too toxic for me to stay in my aunt's house for much longer. There was also no way that I could really see myself going back to live with my father, because after getting raped by Earl, the way I looked at it was like *fuck anybody and everybody,* such as my father, who had ever tried to shit on me or who had ever turned their back on me. I knew that I had to learn how to figure things out on my own and do for myself. I also knew that I would have to somehow strike out on my own and start living on my own.

What I started to do was, whoever I would have sex with or give a blow job to at the sex parties, I would also try to get their phone numbers. That way when I did eventually strike out on my own I would have a readily available list of potential sex clients that I could call on in order to make some money to feed myself and to take care of myself.

In just a matter of three months I had managed to develop a client list of about thirty names. What I would do is call each of my clients once a week or so and act like I was calling just to chit-chat and to also let them know what spot Earl would be taking me to on the weekends. By doing this I began to develop a good rapport with most of my clients and I started getting a lot of repeat business. With those thirty names I felt that I was ready to strike out on my own. In fact, Christmas was about a week or so away and my plan was to bounce a few days after Christmas.

I had met this girl in my school named Tara. Tara was a senior and she was real cool. She gave off that loose whore vibe that was so easy for me to detect. I think it was that vibe that made Tara and me click so well. Well anyway, Tara had hipped me to this older guy that she knew who was a landlord. He rented rooms for like fifty dollars a week. She explained that I would have to share a bathroom and a kitchen with complete strangers but that my room would be my own complete private living space that I wouldn't have to share with anybody.

The fifty dollar price tag sounded right up my alley. I knew that even if my clients proved to be not as reliable as I'd envisioned, I would still be able to make my rent and still have enough money left over to buy some food and to stay fly with my gear.

As it would turn out that plan to move out into my own place would have to be temporarily put on hold.

I had gotten introduced to sex at the age of nine years old. During the five years that passed, considering all of the promiscuous things that I had done and been through, I had been really lucky that I hadn't caught any diseases or gotten pregnant.

Unfortunately for me, though, my number had finally been called. Just before Christmas of 1987 at the tender age of fourteen years old

I found out something that would throw a huge monkey wrench in all of my plans and also really make my life feel like it was a living hell.

What I found out was that I was pregnant.

Yes, pregnant.

Who was the father? I had no idea.

And I also had no idea what the hell I was gonna do about this baby I was carrying.

Part II

The Early Adult Years

Chapter Thirteen

The Dream

It was now the summer of 1991 and I would soon turn eighteen years old.

In between the time when I was pregnant at fourteen and now, a whole lot had taken place. For starters, I had gone back to live with my father shortly after I found out that first time that I was pregnant. I never told anyone about that first pregnancy or the subsequent two others that happened before I graduated from high school. Nor did I ever tell anyone about the abortions that I had gotten in order to cover up my misdeeds.

I had also nixed the idea of moving out on my own simply because by the time I had returned to live with my father he knew that I was old enough to take care of myself and to fend for myself. He had not replaced Vera, the live-in nanny that he had let go shortly after I had gone to live with my Aunt Tanisha. Yeah, when I had returned back to living with my dad, there was no nanny in the house and my father had all but basically moved in with one of his girlfriends in New Jersey who he was really feeling. Needless to say, now that I was getting older, I really hardly ever saw my father. I mean, he would always call to check up on me and make sure there was food in the house, but he was still always MIA.

The way I looked at it, it basically wouldn't have made any sense for me to move out on my own because I practically raised myself all throughout high school.

Earl and I had all but lost contact with each other and I had stopped going to the underground sex parties that he had introduced me to, but I did manage to stay in contact with a lot of my clients that I had met as a result of going to those sex parties. And from that initial list of contacts I was able to get referrals from people who they knew and so my list of clientele grew.

All throughout high school I managed to stay fly and I kept money and was able to buy a nice car when I turned sixteen and it was all as a result of my independent one-girl call-girl service that I had created and was running right from my father's house in Canarsie. And what I liked most was that throughout high school no one really knew what I was doing and how I stayed fly. I mean, I had been close with Tara, the girl that I had met when I was a freshman and she was a senior and she knew what I was into but she'd kept her mouth shut. She probably didn't talk because right after she had graduated from high school she ended up becoming a stripper in order to make money so it was like she and I had this secret life that bonded us. And even though she had graduated a few years before I had, we stayed in touch and we spoke to each other just about everyday and we hung out a lot together even though we both had different hustles.

What was wild and mind-boggling to even me was that with all of the sex that I was having through my call-girl business, when I returned home I had immediately resumed my indulgence into pornography. In fact, it was like my indulgence into watching porn movies and masturbating had greatly increased to the point where I had to start my morning off watching porn and masturbating and when I would come home from school that was what I did. Before I ended my night that was what I did even if sandwiched in-between all of that I had sexed two of my clients it didn't matter, sexually I was just way out of control. It wasn't like I was constantly horny or anything because for the majority of the times it seemed like I would masturbate just for the hell of it.

As far as boyfriends went, I never really had one because I think that subconsciously I had locked up after that experience with BK. I wouldn't allow myself to get that close with anybody else. Besides, I didn't like dealing with the high school dudes who were my age because they were way too immature. I really only dealt with older cats and most of my clients were older so that too made me biased toward older guys.

Right after my graduation—which surprisingly my dad did attend with his girlfriend—I was confused as to what I should do with my life. I mean, a big part of me did want to go to college but at the same time I didn't know if college was for me because I had never given much thought about what I would do as far as a career was concerned.

When I finished high school and the summer vacation started I was sort of in a state of limbo. Was I just gonna try to start working, and if so what the hell was I gonna do, or was I gonna do the college thing?

I was basically confused and I didn't know what to do but one thing that I did do was I kept my call-girl business going. Even that was getting to the point where it was really starting to wear at my spirit. I was really considering stopping it, but the thing was, it was like fucking for money had been woven into my DNA or something so to give it up posed a scary predicament for me.

Then one night in July about three weeks or so after my graduation I had one of the weirdest, realest, and scariest things happen to me that I had ever experienced. It basically changed me and sort of scared me straight and helped me decide on what it was that I should do.

While I slept in my bed it was as if someone had sat down on my bed. I could slightly feel the bed move as their weight pressed onto the mattress. Then it was as if I felt someone gently shaking me and trying to wake me up.

"Shayla," the person called out.

"Shayla, wake up baby," the voice said again as I woke up groggy from my sleep.

"Shayla, baby, it's me," the person said.

I sat up and I kind of got scared because I realized some woman was sitting on my bed. I kind of jumped from being startled.

"Baby, you don't recognize me?"

With my heart pounding I looked at the woman and my mind instantly flashed back to a vision of my mom laying in her casket at her funeral. I knew for sure that it was my mom.

"Mommy?"

"Yes, baby, it's me. It's Mommy."

My heart really started racing with excitement and things just seemed so real to me. At the same time I didn't know if I was dreaming. I didn't think I was dreaming because it was to the point where I could smell the perfume that my mother was wearing. I reached out to see if I could touch her and when I put my arm on her shoulder I really felt her. She grabbed me and pulled me toward her and began hugging me so tight.

"Oh baby, Mommy misses you so much you just don't know!" my mom said as she hugged me.

"I miss you too, Mommy," I said as I sniffed and inhaled some more of my mom's perfume. I couldn't believe that it was really her and that I was actually hugging her and smelling her perfume.

"Shayla, I love you!" my mom stressed to me.

"I love you too," I said as I started crying and holding onto my mom even tighter.

Through my tears I sobbed, and not with anger or bitterness but with just pure, genuine curiosity I asked my mom, "Mommy, why did you leave me?"

There was a pause and I could feel my tears rolling down my face and onto my mom's skin. Then I felt and heard my mom sniffle and I felt one of her tears drip on to me.

Through her tears she said, "Baby, Mommy didn't leave you. There is no way I would have left you. There's no way in the world, baby. Mommy got hurt in a car accident and that's what took me away from you. You understand me, sweetie?"

I couldn't respond because I had missed my mom so much. I was so moved by her presence, I just held her close to me.

"Sweetie, do you?" she asked again.

"Yeah, I understand," I said through my snot and tears.

"Shayla, I did everything that I could to hold on and not leave you. Trust me, I did. And I tried everything to get out of that casket and just hold you when you were at my funeral in your cute little dress, but baby, I just couldn't get to you," my mom said as she wept.

I hated to see my mom cry and I had too much lost time to make up for. The last thing I wanted to do was waste it all on crying.

"It's okay, Mommy, don't cry," I said, sounding as soft and as compassionate as I ever knew I could sound or be.

"Do you believe me?" my mom asked.

"Yes," I replied.

My mom then stood up and she asked me to stand up so she could see me and see how big I'd gotten. What was funny was that as I looked at my mom I might as well have been looking in a mirror because I looked exactly like her.

My mom nodded and started smiling and told me how beautiful I was. Then she pulled me close to her and hugged me again.

"Baby, I don't have that much time so let's sit so I can tell you some things," my mom said as she and I sat back down on my bed.

"First, Shayla, I wanna tell you that you gave me three beautiful grandbabies.They're okay and they're with me, two boys and a girl."

I looked at my mom, kind of confused, and then I realized that she was talking about the three abortions that I had had. My mouth fell open and almost hit the floor.

"It's okay, baby," my mom said as she smiled and stroked my hair.

Then my mom looked at me and I could see her eyes starting to water up. Before long two tears ran down her face, one on each cheek. She held my hands and she said, "Shayla, I want you to know that the things that you were exposed to when you were exposed to them, those things are criminal, and those things made an imprint on your mind and soul. They are horrible and so damaging. Baby, I saw everything, I saw what Joyce did to you, I saw how your dad was, I saw everything baby. It hurt me to no end to not be able to be there to protect you from those things. Understand this, had I been there physically with you, you would not have been exposed to what you were exposed to and things would be different for you, Shayla."

As my mom said those things it was like I couldn't talk or anything. The only thing I could do was just hyperventilate from embarrassment and anxiety and shock all wrapped up in one. The last person that I wanted knowing about my past was my mom, but at the same time she was the person that I wanted to see the most because of my past.

"It's okay, baby, you don't have to be anxious about anything. I love you. I don't have the time right now to explain to you why you have gone through all that you have gone through, but believe me there is gonna come a day when God will make it all clear to you. Before I go, I want you to know that God loves you, your kids love you, and I love you. And baby, you are not a whore! I don't care what anybody tells you, you are beautiful! You hear me?"

"Yes," I said to my mom as I nodded my head and looked at her.

"Shayla, I'm so proud of you and proud that you finished high school and I want you to know something."

"What, Mommy?"

"I want you to go to college and become a doctor," my mom said as she smiled at me.

"Mommy, a doctor?"

"Yes."

My mom paused after she said that and then she told me that she was just being selfish. Me becoming a doctor had always been her dream for me. She wanted me to at least promise her that I would go to college but that I could pursue and become whatever it was that I wanted to become.

"Listen, Shayla, you're gonna get a lot of money from my insurance policy when you turn eighteen and then you're gonna get more money when you turn twenty-one. Please just promise me and make sure that you'll use that money for your education okay?"

"Okay," I told my mom.

My mom and I then just looked at each other and she told me that she was gonna have to go. I begged her to stay and I held onto her as tight as I could.

"It's gonna be all right, sweetie. You'll be fine."

I didn't say anything. I just held onto my mom.

"Shayla, it's gonna be okay, but this is what I want you to promise me as well. I want you to promise me that you'll stop doing what you've been doing with these men. I'm not judging you for it but you're more than that, Shayla. You're beautiful and you're talented and you're gonna be hugely successful. Please stop doing what you're doing. Put away that money that you're gonna get. Don't waste it. Pay for your education with it and save the rest."

I sniffled and I told my mom that she had my word that I would listen to her.

"You're gonna have some more major hurdles come your way, Shayla. In fact, very major hurdles. But no matter what, you make sure that you don't let your past, don't let people, and don't let the negativity that you endure be the things that define you. Let God define you. God loves you and He designed you just as you are for a reason and He thinks you're beautiful. Baby if you don't remember anything else, just remember that you can and you will overcome anything that comes your way but you're gonna have to first forgive and let go. Okay, Shay-shay? You may not understand all of this now but you will as you get older."

"Okay," I said to my mom.

Then she kissed me on my forehead and just like that she was gone.

***

I popped up out of my bed and my heart was pounding.

"Mommy!" I yelled.

I ran frantically out of my room and downstairs yelling for my mom and searching all over the house for her, but I couldn't find her.

I then ran back up into my room and I looked under the bed, out the window, in the closet, everywhere, but I couldn't find my mom.

I was nervous and kind of scared because it was the middle of the night and I didn't know if I had just been dreaming or what. I knew that there was no way that could have been a dream because it was just way too real.

The light was on in my room and I knew that I had not turned it on. Then I smelled my hands and I smelled my nightgown and I smelled the scent of perfume on them both, That same smell of perfume permeated throughout my bedroom and yet I knew that I took a shower before going to bed and hadn't put on any perfume at all.

I wanted to pick up the phone and call my dad but I didn't want him to just brush me off and tell me to go back to sleep.

Then I went into my closet and cleared away some neatly folded clothes that were sitting on top of a black trunk with chrome finishings. I opened up the trunk which contained a bunch of my mother's things from when she was alive. The trunk held pictures and it held some of her clothes and jewelry. It held her wedding gown and newspaper clippings of the car accident that she had been involved in.

As I searched in the box I got the confirmation that I needed. That indeed had been my mom who had visited me. Not only did I find in the trunk the exact outfit that my mom had been wearing but I also found a bottle of perfume. I opened it and sprayed it into the air. Sure enough, it was the exact same fragrance that was on my hand and on my clothes. What was more weird was that trunk that held my mother's things had literally not been opened for about ten years, if not more.

My nervousness started to dissipate because at that point I knew for sure that it had in fact been my mom's spirit that had come to pay me a visit. I smiled a huge Kool-Aid smile and then tears began to run down my cheeks. The only thing that I could do was get on my knees and thank God.

Yeah, I hadn't spoken to God since around the time that my mom had died. Back then when I did speak to Him I would always ask Him, since He could do anything, could He just please bring my mom back to me. When my mom never appeared back in my life I sort of gave up on God. I never found much of a reason to believe in Him considering that He couldn't do such a small thing for me like bring my mother back.

As it turned out, God had heard those numerous prayers of mines from way back in the days and not only had He heard those prayers but on that July night of 1991 He had finally saw fit to answer them.

"Thank you, God," I said as I sat on my bed and relished what I had just experienced.

I was way too hyped and excited to go back to sleep, so I just sat there thinking back on a bunch of things that I had been through in my life.

My mom was right. I was beautiful.

My mom was also right that it was time for me to make some changes in my life. I decided right then and there that I was gonna become a different Shayla Coleman, a Shayla Coleman that my mom would continue to be proud of.

Chapter Fourteen

The Chant

One of the hardest things for me to do was to go cold turkey when it came to stopping my promiscuous activities and stopping my indulgence into porn. Following my mother's visit, I had mustered up the strength to throw away all of my sex clients' phone numbers. I had also changed my phone number so that they wouldn't be able to call me. As for my porno collection, I destroyed all of my porno tapes and all of my magazines. I even threw away my vibrators and sex toys, which was something that I hadn't been without since I was nine years old. Those were just some of the steps that I felt that I needed to take if I was gonna be serious about shifting my lifestyle.

One of the big things that I would have to deal with by going cold turkey was knowing that my money would stop flowing the way I was used to it flowing. I loved buying new clothes and shoes and to say I had a serious shopping habit—well, that was an understatement. As with any habit or addiction it usually has to be financed somehow. With me having decided to shut down my call-girl service I had to figure out a new way to make some money and stay independent.

Really, though, I knew that I would only have to find a way to support my lifestyle for the next two to three months or so. That was because in about a month and a half I was gonna be turning eighteen. I would be receiving the first of two payments of 250,000 dollars which was due me from my mother's insurance policy. I really wasn't stressing it too much because I knew that I would be good real soon.

My friend Tara had been trying for years to get me to strip with her, but stripping was never something that really appealed to me. I mean, don't get me wrong, I had a lot of friends who were strippers and I liked the atmosphere in the strip clubs, but for some strange reason, I never saw stripping as being my cup of tea. Besides, with my decision to change for my mother's sake, I knew that stripping wasn't an option for me.

However, since I liked the atmosphere of the strip clubs and I knew how to fix drinks, I had

Tara put in a good word for me to become a bartender at this strip club in Harlem that she danced at called Pink Chocolate.

With Tara's recommendation I was hired immediately. Despite my age—which I'd used a fake ID to lie about—in late July 1991 I started working as a bartender at Pink Chocolate on Friday, Saturday, and Sunday nights. From my first day I loved my job, which by the way had been my first ever *real* job. The money that I made from tips was one of the main reasons that I liked my job so much.

I made good money from tips for two reasons. The first was because I knew how to talk and bullshit and flirt with all of the horny male customers that would be up in the spot. The second reason was because I made sure that I was always dressed in something provocative that showed a whole bunch of cleavage and was form-fitting.

My flirting, though, was bound to get me in trouble, and about a little more than a month into my job at Pink Chocolate, my mouth as well as my ass had gotten me into a situation where I'd bit off a whole lot more than I could chew.

In most strip clubs there are many dancers who are more than willing to fuck some of the customers that come on to them so long as the

price is right. They go about it in a way that is
discreet enough to not get them bagged for pros-
titution. When alcohol is flowing and chicks are
walking around and dancing half-ass naked and
in some cases butt-ass naked, you better believe
that there is a whole lot of sexual propositioning
going on. As a sexy bartender I wasn't immune to
being propositioned, as was the case on the first
Saturday night in September 1991.

"Yo, you know you a fantasy for most of these
niggas up in here, right?" a cute dark skin customer said to me as I handed him his drink. He
looked pretty familiar but with so many different people passing through that strip club it was
hard to remember every name and every face.

"That's not true," I said as I smiled and asked
the other people at the bar if they needed anything.

"What? You bugging! You know how many
cats would love to leave here witchu right now?"
the guy said over the loud music.

I looked at the guy and smiled again as I took
an order from a different customer for a bottle
of Moët.

After I was done taking the order I sipped on
my own drink. I was already feeling nice from
having smoked some weed about fifteen minutes
prior.

I could feel the dark-skinned guy still looking at me so I looked in his direction. I noticed that an older gentleman was with him and the older guy was whispering something into the cute dark-skinned guy's ear.

"Y'all better not be talking about me," I playfully said to the dark-skinned guy as he sat at the bar.

Liquor and weed always made me horny and at that moment I was starting to get turned on by the way the guy kept licking his lips as he sat at the bar. He wasn't trying to do it in a sensual way or anything like that but it still was a turn-on to me.

"And what if we was talking about you?" the guy said as the other guy who had been whispering something into his ear walked off to a different part of the club.

I looked at the guy but I didn't say anything. I could tell that he wanted me. It was the vibes that he was giving off. I didn't respond to what he had said. Instead, I just listened to hear what he would say next.

"I wanna tell you something," the guy said as he motioned for me to come closer to him so he wouldn't have to holler over the loud music.

"What's up, honey?" I said to him as I leaned in toward him with my boobs practically falling out of my top.

"Me and my man wanna leave with you to-night," the guy whispered into my ear.

I stepped back away from the guy. I didn't smile or say anything. I just remained neutral and sipped on my drink.

The guy looked at me but I was interrupted by someone that wanted to buy a drink.

"I'll be right back," I said to the guy as I whisked away in my high heels and tight jeans and prepared the drink for the other customer.

When I was done I returned back to the guy. Before I said anything I could hear my mother's voice telling me to *just leave that guy alone*. Naturally, I thought about the promise that I had made to leave my promiscuous lifestyle. When that lifestyle came so natural to me and when I had combined the weed and the liquor and the strip-club atmosphere I knew that after only a month or so of being clean I was getting ready to relapse. I could just feel it coming.

"So what's up?" the guy asked me.

I sipped on my drink again and my heart started to pump with nervous anxiety. Out of nowhere I whispered into the guy's ear while the loud music thumped and girls shook their asses in the background, "If you got three hundred for two bottles of Moet then we can make this happen."

The guy looked at me as I stepped away from him. He nodded his head at me to indicate that he had picked up on my double talk.

I walked away from him to go serve other customers and I could have kicked myself for what I had just allowed myself to say.

Shayla, now you acting like a straight ho! Don't take no money from that nigga, I screamed at myself while walking to the other end of the bar.

Yeah, I'm bugging for real. A'ight just leave that nigga down at that end of the bar and forget about it.

That's what I told myself as I worked the other end of the bar. I had no plans of going back and kicking it with the dark-skinned guy but before I could blink he had made his way down to the other end of the bar and was up in my face again.

"Yo, let me get them two bottles," he shouted out to me as he handed me three crisp one-hundred dollar bills.

I looked around to see if any eyes were on me. At that point I knew that I couldn't front on him so I took his money and told him to just chill for a minute.

"So you got us, right?" he asked me.

I nodded my head but verbally I didn't say anything.

It was already a little after three in the morning and the club closed at four.

"You in here 'till it closes or what?"

"Yeah, when it closes I'ma get up outta here," I replied.

"Meet me by the VIP dance area when the music goes off," the guy instructed me.

I nodded my head as I wondered to myself just what the hell I'd gotten myself into.

Shayla, give that nigga his money back and forget about that shit! the angel on my right shoulder said to me.

Just give them niggas some head real quick and keep the money. It's nothing, the devil on my left shoulder said to me.

At that point I could hear my mom's voice again telling me how beautiful I was. I also thought about my three kids that she was raising for me in heaven.

The club was packed to capacity. My services were really needed at the bar but I just felt like I couldn't let my mom down. I knew that she was watching me at that very moment. I found one of the other bartenders and I told her to cover for me because I had to go. I also told one of the owners that I had to bounce and that I would see him tomorrow, even though in my mind I knew that that was gonna be my last night working at that club. I mean, if I really wanted to change, then who was I fooling to think that I could stay in such an environment as a liquor-filled strip club and not get tempted to fuck?

I normally would speak to Tara before leaving to go home but something inside of me was telling me to just hurry the hell up and get outta that spot as quick as I could.

The bad part about Pink Chocolate was that there was only one way in and one way out. When I left I couldn't leave as quick as I'd wanted to because the bouncers wanted to chitchat and kick it with me, while at the same time the entrance was jammed with people trying to enter.

Not tonight. No time to chitchat, Shayla. You gotsta get up outta here quickly, I said to myself. It was so bugged because inside I was panicking to the point where I felt like I was trying to get away from a mugger or a murderer or something.

Thankfully, I made it pretty quickly past the bouncers and the crowd of people trying to get in. I was out the door and heading to my car that was parked three blocks away.

My high heels click-clacked loudly from my brisk walking and as I made it to my car I had never felt so relieved. I couldn't believe how good it felt to finally be able to police myself and show some restraint and self-control. More importantly, I felt good because I knew that I was giving my mom a reason to be proud of me.

I reached inside my Coach bag. I took out my car keys and I unlocked the driver's door to my all-black Saab. Just as I was about get into my car a red Chevy Suburban truck pulled up alongside of my car. It had my car pinned in where even if I wanted to drive off I wouldn't have been able to.

"Yo, where them bottles at?" a male voice said as he got out of the passenger side of the Suburban and ran around to where I was standing.

Ah shit! I said to myself when I realized that it was the same dark-skinned guy from the strip club.

"I still gotchu," I said to the guy as I smiled a nervous smile and thought quick on my feet.

"You still got me? It look to me like you fucking trying to bounce on a nigga!"

"Oh nah, come on, I wouldn't do that. I was just pulling my car around to the front of the club for a better parking spot. I wasn't gonna just bounce on you like that. I gotchu," I said as I nervously chuckled.

The guy looked at me as if he was trying to figure me out as we stood on a dimly-lit and dirty Harlem street.

"Yo, fuck that ho! That bitch is on some bull-shit. I told you she pulled the same shit with me before," the guy that was sitting in the driver's seat of the Suburban said as he got outta the truck and walked up to me.

I had no idea what the hell the guy was talking about and I definitely couldn't place his face.

I didn't say anything but my heart was pounding and I could just sense something wasn't right.

The next thing I know is that the guy who had got out of the driver's seat just smacked the shit out of me and knocked me to the ground.

"Ahh!" I screamed.

I was looking right at the concrete. I was on my hands and knees and my face was stinging like crazy.

The blow had come from out of nowhere and I was shocked. I was even more shocked when I realized that blood was coming from my mouth and dripping onto the concrete.

"What the hell you hit me for?" I screamed as I tried to make it to my feet.

I was smart enough to not go into fight mode because I knew that I couldn't fight off two grown-ass men.

"Shut the fuck up, bitch, and get in this god-damn car!" the guy said as he lifted me off the ground and back onto my feet by yanking my hair.

"Ahh!" I screamed out in genuine pain. "Get off of me!"

"Shut the fuck up," the guy said to me while covering up my mouth.

I was trying to kick and punch and do whatever I could to free myself from the guy's grip. In the process I lost both of my shoes. I screamed at the top of my lungs for somebody to help me, but the street was deserted at 3:30 in the morning.

"Yo, drive the car and I'll stay in the back with this bitch," the guy said as he threw me into the backseat of the roomy old-ass beat-up truck.

I was still kicking and screaming and trying my hardest to fight my way out of that truck.

"Bitch, I said shut the fuck up!" the guy yelled and punched me in my face.

The punch was definitely the hardest punch that I had ever received in my life and it was followed by the guy's large right hand choking the shit out of me.

I couldn't get any air at all and I thought for sure that I was about to die. I scratched and clawed and kicked at the guy, but it was useless. I was pinned on my back and looking up at the guy. I could feel the truck beginning to drive off.

As my eyes were bulging out of my head from the pressure that the guy was applying to my neck, I could tell that he was older and he looked like the fucking devil, but I didn't remember ever seeing him in the strip club before.

"Yo, pull over underneath that overpass by the FDR Drive so we can fuck this ho!" the guy said as he finally loosened his grip from my neck.

"*Hughhhh*," I said as I gasped for air and grabbed my throat to massage the pain.

I soon felt the truck traveling over some real bumpy road that sounded like it was laced with gravel and bricks. Before long it came to a stop and the next thing I know I saw the cute dark-skin turn and look over his shoulder at me from the driver's seat.

"Why you tried to play me? All you had to do was say you wasn't wit' it," the dark-skinned guy said to me.

I shook my head and before I could say anything, the older, devil-looking guy punched me in the face again.

"This is what she do. I told you the bitch took fifty dollars from me before," the guy said as he began ripping at my jeans.

I still had no clue what the guy was talking about and I tried my hardest to fight him off but I didn't have much strength.

"Get the fuck off of me," I yelled as I fought with all I had.

"Y'all gonna rape me? That's some bitch-ass faggot shit," I said as I desperately tried to use reverse psychology, but to no avail.

The guy slapped me again and then he told the dark-skinned guy to come get in the backseat and hold me down so he could fuck me.

The dark-skinned guy quickly climbed over the seat. He was holding my arms down with the force of a bodybuilder. I desperately began to scream my head off for somebody to help me.

"I said shut the fuck up. I'm not gonna tell you that shit again," the older guy yelled as he punched me in my mouth. I could feel loose teeth and blood fall to the back of my throat. I started coughing from nearly choking on my own teeth. The blow had done its job in shutting me up. When I was finally quiet the older guy tore off my jeans while the dark-skinned guy continued to hold my arms down.

"You don't even know who the fuck I am, do you?" the older guy said as he came close to my face with his horrible hot breath, smelling like a wino.

I didn't respond and I just stared at the guy with a look that could kill. I knew I was about to get raped for the second time in my life and at that point I didn't see any sense in resisting. I knew that it was only gonna get me killed or hurt really bad and I wanted it to hurry up and end.

"Look at that pretty little shaved pussy," the guy said as he pulled off his own pants. The musty smell of his dirty-ass dick just about knocked me out.

"Ooooh-weeee. Looka-here, looka-here at this sweet young thang!" he said as he rubbed his hands together like he was about to dig into a Thanksgiving meal.

The guy then rammed his dick inside of me and I let out an excruciating scream.

To shut me up he covered my mouth with one of his hands while he tried his best to fully get himself inside of me.

"Yo, how is that shit?" the dark-skinned guy asked as he continued to hold my arms down.

"For some ho pussy, this some tight good pussy right here," the older guy said as he grunted and pumped himself in and out of me while his disgusting sweat dripped down from his head and onto my face.

"Look at me and tell me who I am," he screamed at me as he continued to ram himself inside of me.

I looked at the guy and the only image that came to my mind was that of my cousin Earl when he was raping me in his basement.

"I'm that nigga you tried to get over on in Queens that time," the guy said while not breaking stride and still digging into me.

Through the intense pain that I was feeling I then refocused my eyes on him and my eyes got wide as hell.

"Yeah, you remember me now, right bitch?" the guy said to me.

At that point it hit me. I did in fact remember him. I couldn't believe that he was the same older guy that I had gotten the fifty dollars from that first night that I had gone to an underground sex party with Earl. I had taken his fifty dollars but for different reasons he had never gotten any sex out of me that night. Now four years later I couldn't believe that not only had he remembered me, but he was actually raping me. It was by far the worst position that I'd ever found myself in.

Realizing who this guy was, it caused something to snap. I lost it and started fighting again to free myself.

It was no use as the two guys were too much for me.

"I ain't raping you. Bitch, I paid for this pussy two times and both times you tried to play me," the guy barked at me as he continued pumping in and out of me.

He then moved his face close to mine. In my left ear he grunted and moaned as he began to chant, "I'm gonna hit this pussy and hit it raw. I'm gonna hit this pussy 'till its sore!"

I couldn't take it and I felt like I was gonna pass out from the pain and the humiliation and the guilt for having let my mom down. I also couldn't take it because in my mind I was going crazy. I was going crazy as I started to think that I deserved to be getting raped and treated like I was being treated. After all, maybe he was right, maybe it wasn't rape, maybe he was just collecting on what I had allowed him to pay me for but had never given to him.

Indian giver! Indian giver! Shayla is an Indian giver! my mind shouted to me in the teasing voice of a small child.

Right then and there I just went limp. I didn't care what happened from that point on, I just wanted everything to end. I don't remember much else of what happened. The last things I do remember is the guy's sweat dripping directly into my mouth and him grunting and moaning in my other ear, my right ear this time.

He laughed and then repeated in my right ear the same chant that he had just said to me in my left ear. Only this time I remember feeling his hot liquor breath burning a hole into my skin as he repeatedly chanted, "I'm gonna hit this pussy and hit it raw. I'm gonna hit this pussy 'till it's sore!"

Wake up Shayla, wake up! I screamed to myself.

Unfortunately this wasn't a dream. It was a nightmare and I was living through it.

Yup, it was as real as real can get.

Chapter Fifteen

Still Lying

Apparently after I had been raped, I was driven near the Fifty-ninth Street Bridge and just dumped on the side of the road like a sick puppy. I say *apparently* because I don't remember being dumped there but I was told by the cops and doctors that that is where a concerned passerby saw my shoeless urine-soaked half-naked unconscious body and called 911 to get me some help.

What's funny is that the two guys that raped me had raped me not too far from 125th Street and the FDR Drive in Harlem. Had they chosen to dump my unconscious body anywhere in those uptown blocks above Ninety-sixth Street, I probably would have been either left for dead or taken to some police precinct and locked up overnight for indecent exposure or something like that. Since my attackers had been *gracious* enough to dump me in the more upper-class part of town it resulted in a totally different outcome.

For starters I was taken to Bellevue Hospital, one of the finest hospitals in New York City, as opposed to being taken to Harlem Hospital, one of the worst hospitals in New York City. Thus I received some of the best treatment imaginable. Being found near the Fifty-ninth Street Bridge also managed to shine a huge spotlight on me and the vicious crime that had been lavished upon me. If this could happen to me in a white part of town then that meant that it could also happen to a white woman in that same white part of town. Therefore, all of the authorities took this seriously. They made it a priority to find out who had violated me and how quickly could that person or persons be apprehended and brought to justice.

Once the media got wind that an innocent seventeen-year-old girl from Brooklyn had been brutally raped and left for dead in an expensive part of town on the east side of Manhattan, all hell broke loose.

I vaguely remember being inside of an ambulance but I do remember being wheeled into the hospital emergency room. I heard the cops telling the paramedics and the doctors that the media would more than likely be converging on the hospital in a short period of time and that the doctors were not to say anything to the media about me or my condition, especially not until my parents had arrived at the hospital.

"Ms. Coleman, hi, I'm Detective Pelonis and this is my partner, Detective Mangini," the two female detectives said to me as I lay on a gurney and had doctors working on me and sticking shit inside of my veins

"Detective, with all due respect, can we just stabilize the patient before you start with the questions?" the doctor said to the detective.

"Doctor, with all due respect to you, you do your job and you let us do our job," Detective Pelonis said.

The doctor and the detective looked at each other and then they both started to speak to me at the same time. The detective was asking me did I mind telling her what had happened to me and the doctor was telling me what to expect and that she would be doing a vaginal exam, but that she first wanted me to change into a hospital gown.

All the talk was like noise to me. I was still feeling really groggy and my head was spinning from all of the things being thrown at me.

Thankfully, the doctor tuned out and allowed the detective to take the lead. She told the nurses to just wait until the detectives were done before proceeding.

"Ms. Coleman, I know you don't feel too good and I'll be as brief as possible, but I need to ask you certain questions so that we can determine exactly what happened to you and exactly who did this to you," the detective said.

I just looked at the detective but I didn't respond.

"Can you tell me what happened?" the detective asked.

I looked at her and just gave her this blank stare. I was in a lot of pain and I was also confused and trying my hardest to figure out just what I should say.

"Shayla?" the detective said to me.

She then took hold of my hand to make me feel more comfortable.

"I was in Times Square," I said and then I paused because it felt funny to talk, being that my upper front teeth had been knocked out.

The detective nodded her head for me to continue as she scribbled down notes on her pad.

"My birthday is in a few days, so me and my friend went there to hang out to celebrate my birthday."

The detective feverishly continued to scribble down everything that I was saying.

"Who is your friend?" she asked me.

"Tara," I replied and simultaneously I started coughing.

"Okay," the detective said.

"We just went to the movies and then we hung out in Times Square just walking around taking pictures and stuff. I had drove and we were ready to leave and go home. When we were walking back to the car these guys that we had met in the movie theater, they saw us and came up to us and started harassing us because we wouldn't give them our phone numbers," I lied and said.

The detective then asked me what street was I parked on, she asked me to fully describe the guys, did I know the guys, what movie did we see, where did Tara live, and did I have her phone number. She really pressed me when I told her that the guys had put me inside their truck.

I lied and answered most of the detective's questions but when she pressed me on where Tara lived, what happened to Tara, and Tara's phone number that was when I broke down and started crying and told the detective that I really didn't want to talk anymore.

"Detective?" the doctor said in a sarcastic way.

"Okay, thank you, Shayla. Listen, we're gonna either stop back by later on or have you come by the precinct to look at some photos to see if you recognize who did this to you."

I nodded my head and then the detective asked me one last question about Tara. She wanted to know if Tara had also been put inside the truck with me and raped.

"Well, look at my teeth. All I remember was fighting and getting punched in my face repeatedly. It was like I would black out and come to and black out again so honestly I don't even remember what happened with Tara."

The detective scribbled everything down and she looked at her partner. Then they both thanked me and told me to try not to worry about anything and that I would be okay. They assured me that they would catch the people who had done this to me.

As soon as the detectives left, the doctors went to work on me, checking me out from head to toe and swiping me with Q-tips and all kinds of swabs. Before they could fully finish examining me, my father and his girlfriend came into my room.

"Oh my God! Shayla, are you okay?" my father asked with genuine-sounding concern.

I shook my head *no* and then I started balling in order to really play it up and get his sympathy.

My father's girlfriend hugged me and rubbed my face.

"Baby, what happened?" my father asked me.

"Sir, I understand you're concerned, but please just let us finish examining her and you'll be able to talk to her," the doctor said very compassionately but very firm.

My father and his girlfriend were asked to wait out in the hallway while the doctor and the nurses finished examining me.

The tears that I had mustered up for dramatic effect had ceased rolling from my eyes. I laid there and continued to be examined. While laying there I realized that I had to keep lying and that I couldn't tell anyone what had really happened to me because how would I explain the fact that I was in a strip club tending bar at seventeen years old? I also knew that I would have to get in touch with Tara as soon as possible and have her play along with my Times Square story.

The media got ahold of this whole rape that had happened to me, and while the doctors and the cops had assured me that no one would be allowed to leak my name to the public, even with my anonymity I still wondered just how long I would be able to keep the lie going about what had really happened to me?

Since I was young I had been used to lying to cover up misdeeds and shit that I had no business being involved in. Even though I had been brutally raped and there was now this big spotlight that was gonna be shined on me, I didn't care. I was gonna keep lying for as long as I had to in order to cover my ass.

The Times Square thing was the story that I had come up with and that was the story that I was gonna be sticking to 'till the end.

Chapter Sixteen

No Love Like A Father's Love

As soon as I was discharged from the hospital I had two uniformed police officers waiting to escort me and my father down to the police precinct to look at mug shots. His girlfriend followed behind us in my father's car.

I was feeling horrible and with three of my top front teeth missing I looked like a hot mess. The only thing I wanted to do was see a dentist as soon as possible so I could replace my lost teeth.

On the way to the precinct as we sat in the back of the patrol car, I couldn't believe that my father had actually put his arm around me, hugged me, kissed me on the cheek, stroked my hair, and told me that he loved me.

His signs of affection had shocked the hell out of me, but what was more shocking was that it really seemed genuine. It had taken a brutal rape for me to finally get that type of attention from him, but I was just glad to be getting it and it made me feel really good.

When we arrived at the precinct I was still wearing hospital-issued garb and slippers along with a thin jacket that my father's girlfriend had let me borrow. My clothes had to be held as evidence and sent down to the police crime lab.

Anyway, at the precinct I was met by two different New York City detectives, both of whom were men. I was also met by a female prosecutor from the district attorney's office as well as a male investigator from the district attorney's office.

Along with my father and his girlfriend—who everyone took as my mom—we all went into a room. The new detectives, the investigator and the prosecutor all took turns asking me basically the same questions that the female detectives had asked me earlier when I was at the hospital.

I answered all of their questions and I made sure that I was consistent with what I had said earlier to the other detectives at the hospital. The only time that I appeared to get flustered was when they would press me on information about Tara. They couldn't believe that I didn't have a phone number for her or an address for her.

"I have her number programmed into my cordless phone at home. I just press one button and it dials her, so I never actually dial her number. That's why I don't know it off the top of my head," I lied.

"But what about where she lives? A last name, maybe?" the detectives pressed me.

"She lives all the way in Queens and I live in Brooklyn. That's too far to be traveling so usually what we do is we meet up at wherever we're going out to. Like that night we met up at the movie theater on Forty-second Street in Times Square."

Everyone in the room looked at each other without saying anything, then the prosecutor suggested that we look at some mug shots to see if I could see anyone who looked familiar.

"Mr. Coleman, I know it has been an extremely long and difficult day for both you and your daughter, but we just want her to look at these photos while things are still fresh in her mind. After this she is free to go and we'll follow up tomorrow," the prosecutor said as my father nodded his head.

For about a half an hour I looked through book after book of mug shots and none of the faces looked familiar. Finally when I was combing through what had to have been the tenth book of mug shots I did see a face that looked similar to the older guy that assaulted me.

"I think this is him," I said out loud.

Everyone in the room scrambled and hovered over me and around me to get a better look at the photo.

"That motherfucker! I'll kill his ass!" my father shouted in anger.

"Mr. Coleman," the prosecutor said in a stern voice.

My father apologized but he kept a look on his face that said he wanted to kill.

"Now, Shayla, are you sure? Look again real closely," the detectives said to me.

I studied the picture for another thirty seconds or so and I was certain that it was the guy.

"I can tell by his eyes and that same rough-looking, thin grayish beard," I said.

"Beautiful," the investigator from the district attorney's office replied.

The detectives said that they would get to work on it right away.

At that point I was more than ready to get the hell out of there so I could make contact with Tara and also have my father make arrangements for me to see a damn dentist.

Everyone milled about for a few more minutes and the prosecutor made small talk with my father. Then thankfully we were ready to go.

"Shayla, it's very important that you have Tara call us as soon as you make contact with her," the investigator from the district attorney's office said.

I assured him that I would.

"Try to get some rest and I promise you we're gonna get the people who did this to you," the prosecutor said to me as she hugged me.

My father let his girlfriend drive home and he sat in the backseat with me. For the first time in my life I saw tears fall out of my father's eyes. He hadn't even cried at my mother's funeral, yet he was crying as we drove home.

"What's wrong, Daddy?" I said as I couldn't believe how it melted me to see my dad in tears.

"I just feel like I failed you," my father said to me. "Shit like this ain't supposed to happen. I'm supposed to be there to protect you," my father screamed as he banged his fist against the headrest that was in front of him.

I hugged my father and I told him that it wasn't his fault and that I would be okay.

There was this moment of eerie silence as I just held on to my father like I was holding on for dear life. I could actually feel his chest rising and falling as we hugged each other. I had never been that close to him and I didn't want to let go. I actually felt like a little school-age girl at that moment.

"I'm not crying, so you don't need to shed no tears," I reassured my dad while his girlfriend kept quiet and maneuvered her way across the Brooklyn Bridge.

"You don't understand, Shayla," my father said as he shook his head and looked at me in the face with teary eyes. "I just feel like I failed you."

I pulled back slightly from my father and I looked in his eyes. It was like I could see into his soul at that moment and I could see what his spirit was saying. I could just tell that he wished he had been there to protect me from the people that assaulted me, but I also knew that his words held much deeper meaning.

For the first time I felt like my father wasn't completely clueless to how I had been living. Now there was no way in hell that he knew everything, but I think he had to know that I had some whorish tendencies. I think that at that moment he was admitting his responsibility and guilt for some of my promiscuity. Although he didn't say it verbally I knew that he knew it was ultimately my promiscuity that had put me in the position that I was in.

Inside, I just wanted to let out the biggest sigh of relief because it felt so good that my father actually cared about me. He actually cared enough to cry.

Funny thing was that when I saw him crying it actually made me feel guilty. It's hard to explain why, but I just felt guilty and so I decided to focus on something different.

"Daddy, the only thing you should be crying about is my teeth! Look at me. I look like Mike Tyson got ahold of me or something," I said as I shook my head.

My father clenched his teeth with anger. He pulled me close to him and told me not to worry. He promised me that he would make sure that he hooked me up with a good dentist and that I would be looking as good as new in about a week.

"Okay," I said as I nestled my head into my daddy's chest and snuggled up next to him for the rest of the ride home.

Chapter Seventeen

Get Your Lies Straight

It had taken me all night to finally get ahold of Tara. From the moment that I walked in my house I had been repeatedly calling her crib trying to get ahold of her but her phone just kept ringing out to voice mail. Finally at around ten o'clock that Sunday night I managed to get ahold of her.

"Tara, where you been?"

"Excuse me?" Tara replied.

"I been calling you forever and you ain't been picking up your phone."

"Shayla? You sound different."

"Yo listen, I sound like this because I got into a situation last night when I left the club," I said, trying not to talk too loud so that my father wouldn't overhear me.

"Yeah, what happened to you? I looked around one minute and saw you and the next minute you was gone. What kinda situation you talking about?"

I got up from off of my bed and closed my bedroom door to give myself some more privacy.

"Last night when I left the club these dudes that I had been flirting with, they see me as I'm getting ready to get into my car, and they snatched my ass up, beat the shit outta me, and raped me."

"Shayla, I know you bullshitting, right?"

"No. I'm dead serious. The reason I sound different is because my front teeth got knocked the fuck out and all of that."

"Oh my God! Shayla, why didn't you wait for me last night and why are you just calling me now? I can't believe what you telling me. Girl, don't you know we don't never leave the club alone? I don't care if you was just bartending. You know the rules."

"Tara, I know, I know. But listen, this is the thing, now I gotta talk low and I gotta talk quick because I don't want my father to hear what I'm saying, so I'm gonna need you to just follow me. A'ight?"

"Yeah, yeah."

"Now this is the thing. There was two dudes, and one of the dudes had already paid me three hundred dollars when we was in the club. I had told him that I would get with him and his boy. Then I just changed my mind—I mean, you know what I told you about how my moms had came to me in the dream and all of that. Well, that was playing in the back of my mind so I was like, nah, I can't do this. So instead of giving the money back, I just bounced up outta the spot with their dough, and the thing was I wasn't trying to get over on them or anything like that. It's just that I got scared and my mind was bugging out so I just bounced."

"Okay, I gotchu so far, keep going," Tara said to me.

"So I make it to my car but before I could get in and pull off the same two dudes from the club pull up alongside of me and they heated because I just bounced on them. So before you know it I'm in they truck getting my ass beat and raped!" I blew out some air from my lungs and shook my head.

"Shayla, you ain't bullshitting about this, are you?"

"Girl, I'm dead-ass serious! But now this is the thing. I told the cops a whole other story. Tara, you know I wasn't suppose to be working up in the club that night so I couldn't tell them about that. I gave them this story about how me and you went to the movies in Times Square and—"

"*Me and you*? Shayla, you put my name in this?"

"Tara, I had to."

"Yo, Shayla, that is some serious shit. What the hell?"

"Tara, just listen."

I went on to tell Tara exactly what I had told the detectives and I begged for her to go along with my story. She was very reluctant because she feared that she would get locked up if it were ever proven that she was lying.

"Tara, trust me on this."

"Shayla, you my girl and all, but I ain't trying to go to jail for yo ass."

I sighed into the phone and tried to figure out just what the hell to say in order to convince Tara to go along with my story.

"Tara, the cops is pressing me for your info. Girl, you gotta back me on this."

Tara blew a lot of air into the phone but she didn't say anything.

"Okay, look. Remember the money that I told you I was gonna be getting when I turned eighteen? Listen, if you back me on this I swear on my mother's grave that I'll give you fifteen thousand dollars cash straight up no chaser."

"What?"

"Yes, fifteen thousand dollars cash. Tara, come on! I need you to do this for me."

Tara was silent for about a minute or so. I also kept silent, waiting for her response.

She finally broke the silence and said, "Shayla, word is bond, I'll do this but if you don't come through with that bread I'm fucking snitching on you to save my ass. I'm just being straight real and upfront witchu. I mean, I love you and all but I ain't trying to risk going to jail for you and not get nothing out of it in the process."

"No. Tara, I got you, don't worry about that. As soon as I get my money I'll hit you off. You got my word on that."

Tara continued to have some reservations, but I made sure that she was straight on every aspect of the story and what we would say so not to contradict one another. I even gave her detailed descriptions of the two men who had raped me and we repeatedly went over their descriptions. The main thing that we had to get down was what had happened to her that allowed her to not be accosted when I was and if she had managed to get away, then why didn't she call the cops on my behalf?

"All you gotta say is that we both were trying to fight them off and get them to stop harassing us. You managed to break free and you ran and just kept running until you were able to get into a yellow cab. You didn't call the cops because you were safe at that point and you weren't sure as to what had happened to me. You assumed that I had managed to break free and run to safety as well."

Tara sighed into the phone after I had finished talking.

"And just tell them you repeatedly called my crib and you didn't reach me, but you didn't go to the cops because you continued to assume that I was okay."

"Shayla, I don't know if that's gonna cut it. They're gonna see right through that shit. What if I don't pick the guy out in the mug shots like you did? Then what?"

"That's the thing, you don't have to pick anybody out. Look through all of the books and just say that you don't recognize anybody from the photos."

Tara was still reluctant but she was my girl so she decided to go through with it. When I hung up the phone with her I immediately went to my father and told him that I had just spoken to her and that she was okay and had not been hurt. I then suggested that he call the precinct and relay the info about Tara as far as her phone number, address, and all of that.

I was doing the best I could to cover my tracks and hoping like hell that me and Tara had our lies straight because if we didn't, I would surely be exposed as just some lying-ass underage ho who had tried to get over on some dude only to have my scam backfire on me.

Chapter Eighteen

Reasonable Doubt

A little more than a week had passed since I had been raped. During that time a whole lot had taken place. For starters, I had made it to a cosmetic dentist and got my teeth fixed, so my appearance was tight and back up to par. I had also turned eighteen years old. Three days after I'd turned eighteen I received a check for 250,000 dollars which was due to me from my mom's life insurance policy.

As for my rape case, the detectives and the district attorney had repeatedly questioned Tara as to what had happened that night. Although Tara and I had rehearsed our story as well as we could, a whole lot of doubts were being raised and cast upon the credibility of my allegations.

Behind the scenes, the cops and the district attorney were putting all kinds of pressure on me and Tara. Thankfully, my father was there ridin' with me the whole time and because of his presence he didn't allow the cops and their questioning to spook me. At the same time I could sense that even my father was starting to doubt what I had alleged.

On one particular occasion they had separated Tara and myself. They questioned us and had us recount for them everything that had transpired on the night of the rape. Then they brought us into a room together and questioned us some more to see if our stories were still lining up.

"Shayla and Tara, here's the deal. We want to believe everything that you two are telling us but at the same time you two have got to be straight-up with us. We have a man that we are ready to move on and bring into this station for questioning but before we do that you two gotta tell us what *really* went down that night," the female detective who had originally taken my story at the hospital said to me as she paced back and forth in a small closed-door room that we were in.

"Detective Pelonis, we told you what went down. Why would we lie about that? You seen how messed-up my face looked. The doctors confirmed that I was raped. So what else is there to say?" I vented to her.

The detective sat down and pulled her chair next to Tara and me. "Look. I'm not trying to come across harsh or anything like that and I sympathize with what happened to you two that night. But what I'm saying is that there are a few holes in what you two have been telling me and we need to clear them up."

"Holes like what?" I replied.

The detective then reached into her pocket. "Well for starters, this is the driver's license that the paramedics found on your possession."

I looked at the fake driver's license that I had totally forgotten about.

"And Tara, if this is not you then you have a twin sister out there who looks a whole lot like you," the detective added as she placed a promotional postcard from Pink Chocolate on to the table, which had Tara's face and half-naked body on it.

Tara was silent and I didn't say anything.

The assistant district attorney was also in the room and so was my father. My father didn't say anything but he came close and he examined the fake driver's license as well as the Pink Chocolate postcard. The assistant district attorney, however, did speak up.

"Here is the thing. Shayla, we're gonna bring this guy in that you picked out of the mug shots and if one of you are able to pick him out of the lineup and he doesn't have an alibi, then we're gonna arrest this guy. The media and everyone is putting pressure on us to solve what happened to you and we wanna solve it. But at the same time, if we arrest this guy and it goes to trial, anything and everything about the both of you, in terms of your past, is gonna come into question. So what we're saying is, if you're holding something back from us out of fear or whatever the case may be, just tell us now before you get exposed later at a much higher consequence."

Tara looked at me and I could tell that she was nervous as hell, but I was praying that she would just hold her ground and not admit to shit.

I kept my mouth shut and looked at Tara and then I looked straight ahead and just stared at the wall in silence.

"Shayla, what about the driver's license?" my father spoke up and said.

I gave him a look as if to say, *nigga, whose side are you on?*

I sucked my teeth and then sighed and said, "Everybody has a fake ID."

The assistant district attorney looked at me and said, "Shayla, this is not about everybody, it's about you. And what's gonna happen is when it comes out that you were walking with a fake ID on the night you were raped, then that is gonna make everything else you say questionable."

"Look. All I know is what I told you that happened. And why does that gotta come out now, anyway? I thought my identity was gonna be protected."

Detective Pelonis then spoke up and said, "Shayla, your identity will be protected. Don't worry about that. Now here's the thing, and I can't shoot any straighter than this. Tara, my partner and I took a trip over to Pink Chocolate and they confirmed that you do work there as a stripper. So what's the story?"

"I'm a dancer, not a stripper," Tara blurted out as she rolled her eyes.

The detective cracked a half smile and then she continued on. "No one at Pink Chocolate would say whether or not you were working there on the night that Shayla was raped. I have enough experience to know that they were probably just covering for you. But you better believe that if we arrest this guy, the picture is gonna be painted that the two of you are nothing more than loose strippers, walking around with fake ID's, who, if they got raped it probably wasn't rape and they probably deserved it."

"Now wait a minute, now," my father said, speaking up. "My daughter may have had a fake ID but—"

The detective cut my father off and said that in no way was she trying to label me and Tara. She just wanted us to be aware of the realities of what could come. The assistant district attorney pointed out that if things were to go to a trial down the road and if concrete evidence was presented to contradict my story and Tara's story, then we could both be looking at perjury charges. She stated that it was highly unlikely, but that they had to let us know the real deal.

I sat stoned-face. I decided to just think about my 250,000 dollar check that I was waiting to clear in my bank account that I had just recently opened up.

Thankfully, the mini-interrogation was soon over and the cops let us go. As we walked out of the precinct I could just tell that everyone—including my father—had high reasonable doubt as to my account of what had happened that night, but like I had said to myself earlier, that was my story and I was sticking to it.

As it turned out, the next day the cops did arrest the guy that I had picked out of the mugshot books. His name was Antonio Reid and he was forty-four years old, which was about the age I would have guessed from looking at the guy that night when he assaulted me.

The cops were ready to bring Antonio Reid into a lineup with five other men who they had chosen at random. They wanted me to go first and then Tara to see if one of us could pick him out of the lineup.

I wasn't too nervous but at the same time there was a sense of anxiety running through me. I mean, even though none of the suspects could see me through the doubled mirror partition that separated us, I guess the nervousness was from the thought of being in such close proximity to the man who had violated me.

Well, as the men were brought in one by one and stood in their respective places I examined each one of their faces. It didn't take me long to know which one of the guys it was.

"It's number five," I said in all of about ten seconds after the last guy was brought in.

"Are you sure?" the detective asked. "You didn't really look for that long."

"I'm sure it's number five. All he did was clean his self up and shave his nappy-ass face hair," I said in a confident, matter-of-fact tone.

The detectives looked at each other and smiled but they didn't say anything.

"Well, is that him?" my father asked.

"We got him," the detectives replied.

"You motherfucking bastard!" my father had screamed at the guy even though the guy couldn't see us and I don't think that he could hear us either.

My father then grabbed me and hugged me and told me that he loved me and was proud of me for being so strong.

Right after that my dad and I were ushered out of the room and Tara was brought into the room. Tara was in the room much longer than I had been but when she came out she emerged with a smile.

"I picked the right guy," she said to me as she hugged me. She held onto me and she playfully whispered into my ear, "I want all large bills for all of this stress you puttin' a sister through."

The detectives took our hugging and smiling as us being relieved that we had picked the right suspect out of the lineup.

"So what happens now?" my father asked.

The detectives said that they were gonna place Antonio Reid under arrest and question him at length and then put him through the system.

I definitely was relieved because I was sure that a lot of the doubt that I know had been in the detectives' heads was now starting to dissipate just a bit. At the same time, I was relieved because picking the right guy out of the lineup also helped reassure me that I was not just some ho who was concocting a story. Nah, I was a beautiful human being who had been assaulted and raped.

The next day I received a call from the assistant district attorney and she asked me if I was sitting down.

"No, I'm not."

"Well, you have to sit down for this because you won't believe it."

"Okay. I'm sitting," I said even though I was still standing and pacing the floor with my cordless phone.

"Wait, wait—before you say anything, is it good news or bad news?"

She chuckled and told me that it was definitely good news.

"A'ight cool. Well then what's up?" I asked.

"You and Tara said that you two had gone to see the movie *Terminator 2*. Is that right?"

"Yeah," I replied.

"Well, Antonio Reid gave a videotaped confession to the police last night and he admitted to being in Times Square on the night that you were assaulted and he even admitted to seeing *Terminator 2*!"

My heart skipped a beat and my mouth fell open because I knew that the chances were very slim that that could have actually happened, because Antonio Reid was at the strip club in Harlem that night, unless he had been in Times Square prior to coming to Pink Chocolate.

"He admitted that?" I asked.

"Yes, and he voluntarily admitted it. It was like that was the alibi that he gave for his whereabouts. He's even saying that his fiancée was with him at the movies that night and he can have her back up what he's saying.

"Wow," I said, meekly.

"Shayla, this is open-and-shut. He has an attorney and they've agreed to provide a hair and blood sample and if that comes back positive, I don't even think that this case will go to trial. He'll probably take a plea deal and go to jail. The guy is a two-time felon with a previous conviction for assault and another separate conviction for weapons possession."

I really didn't know what to say, but I could tell that the assistant district attorney's confidence level in me and my story had grown and any reasonable doubt that her or the cops may have had was now gone.

The only thing now was that it was me, Shayla Coleman, who was the one with the reasonable doubt.

Chapter Nineteen

Crocodile Tears

Two days after Antonio Reid had admitted to being in Times Square on the night I was raped, Tara and I found ourselves in Citibank. My check had cleared and the money was to become available to me that day.

"Is this sick or what?" I asked Tara as I showed her my checking account balance that was on the ATM screen.

"Damn girl! You fucking rich," Tara said to me as she laughed.

I smiled and the two of us proceeded to walk into the bank so that I could withdraw the money that I had promised to her.

"So what you gonna do with all that cash?" Tara asked me.

"I'm getting an all-white baby Benz," I replied without hesitation.

"That's it?"

"Nah, of course not, and after that, I'm doing whatever the hell I wanna do when the fuck I wanna do it. You know what I'm saying?" I said to Tara as I slapped her five.

"I know that's right."

The two of us reached the teller's window and I handed the teller my withdrawal slip along with my ID. She looked at me, looked at my ID, and then she asked me how did I want my money.

"What the fuck you mean, how do I want my money?" I barked at the lady.

Tara then discreetly explained to me that I had the option of taking large bills like hundreds and fifties versus small bills like twenties and tens.

"Oh well, why didn't she say that, then? Give me all hundreds."

The teller rolled her eyes. She walked away for a minute and then she soon came back with a wad of money. I was withdrawing 20,000 dollars so the teller counted off 200 one-hundred-dollar bills.

"Can you do me a favor and put fifteen thousand in one pile and five thousand in another pile?" I asked her.

She looked at me and nodded, but she didn't say anything.

"This bitch got an attitude," I said to Tara underneath my breath.

Tara smiled and told me to just chill.

Not much long after that, the teller handed me two envelopes full of cash. I handed Tara the envelope that had the most cash and I took the smaller envelope. Just like that my account had dwindled down to 230,000.

"Don't this make you wanna cum on yourself just looking at all this cash?" I asked Tara.

"You ain't say nothing but a word," Tara replied.

"Now did I keep my promise or what?" I said.

"You my fucking girl goddammit," Tara shouted into the car as she slapped me five. "We gotta go out tonight and just live it up and celebrate."

Tara was right. I had been through a lot over the past few weeks and I deserved to do something nice for myself. After all, I had never even really gotten the chance to celebrate my eighteenth birthday, and with a bank account full of money, what better time to celebrate?

Tara and I made plans to hook up with each other later that evening. We would finalize then just where we were gonna be hanging out. Before we parted ways, I made sure that I told Tara to not tell anyone how much money I was holding. She swore to me that she wouldn't and she made me swear to her that I would never say anything to anyone about her lying to the cops for me.

That, of course, was without question, because if I did say anything to someone else then I would only be setting myself up for a problem.

By the time I had returned back home from the bank it was still early in the day on a Thursday morning. I was actually surprised that my father was still in the crib when I got there. Lately he had been hanging out around the house a lot more. I didn't think much of it and I just attributed his renewed presence to the fact that I had been raped and him wanting to make me feel more secure following such an ordeal. However, as I would quickly find out, that had not been the true reason he had been hanging around.

"Hey, baby girl," my father said to me as I walked into the kitchen.

Baby girl? I said to myself. *Where in the hell did that pet name come from?*

"Hey," I said as I proceeded to fix myself something to eat.

"Shayla, you know I been meaning to speak to you about something for some time now. I guess now is as good a time as any."

I got two eggs from the refrigerator, cracked them, and put them in a bowl.

"Okay," I said to my father as I scrambled the eggs and prepared to cook them.

"Well, I never told you any of this because to me it didn't seem right to worry you or burden you with my financial problems."

I turned on the fire, placed a skillet and some butter on the fire, and looked at my father so he could continue on.

"What I'm trying to say is, ever since your mom died, I've made some horrible decisions with my money. I got myself into some trouble. I'm over my head in debt, with bills and credit cards. I refinanced this house a couple of times and the bank won't let me borrow any more money against it. Right now I'm so far behind in the mortgage that they about to foreclose on me and take this house from *us*."

I poured my eggs into the skillet and began to cook them. My mind was racing and I didn't exactly know what to say. A little voice inside of me was telling me to be smart and be careful.

"So what are you saying, exactly?"

"What I'm saying is I know you just got the money from your mom's insurance policy. That's your money and you can do whatever it is that you wanna do with it. What I wanna ask you, Shayla, is to loan me one hundred and twenty-five thousand dollars so I can take that and pay off the house. Then we won't have to worry about a foreclosure or anything like that, and I won't have as much pressure on me."

My eggs were just about ready. I liked my eggs to be really runny so I never let them cook for too long.

"One hundred and twenty-five thousand? Wow, that's a lot."

"Shayla, I know it is. But it's only half of what you got, plus you're gonna get another two hundred and fifty thousand dollars when you turn twenty-one," my father said in a tone that sounded like he was desperate and trying to convince me.

I sat down at the table and began eating my eggs. I told my father that I could give him something, but I had to think about giving him 125,000.

"You gotta think about it?"

"Yeah, I mean I could give you like five thousand, but—"

"Five thousand? Shayla, you got two hundred and fifty fucking thousand dollars! I'm asking you for help and that's the best you can do? I don't believe this shit," my father screamed.

The next thing I knew my father grabbed my plate of food and snatched the fork out of my hand and flung them both across the kitchen. The eggs, the plate, and the fork all slammed into the kitchen wall and crashed to the floor, making a huge mess.

"You gonna eat my fucking food in my fucking kitchen and you got the audacity to sit in my face and tell me you can't help me out? Shayla, after all I did for you. You gotta be fucking kidding me?"

"Daddy, why are you cursing like that? Calm down," I said as I stood up from the kitchen table.

"Don't tell me to fucking calm down and don't act like you got virgin ears, Shayla."

"You know what?" I said as I shook my head and walked out of the kitchen.

My father continued to rant and rave and I couldn't believe how mad he had gotten. He was slapping things as he walked by them and just grunting and venting to himself like a spoiled child.

I made it up to my room and sat on my bed. I didn't know what to do. Part of me started telling myself to just give him the money and forget about it. Another part of me had no way of knowing if he was telling the truth or not. Even if he was, how in the hell did I know what he was really gonna do with the money after I'd given it to him?

I sat and thought for a few minutes. As I sat, I got kind of angry. Not violent angry, but pissed-off angry. I realized that all of that money that

I had gave me a sense of power in that no one could have control over me like they could when I was younger and dependent on other people. I was eighteen with money and old enough to call my own shots. I had to go let my father know what was what.

I walked back downstairs and I confronted him.

"Daddy, I just gotta tell you something. Understand that I am not trying to disrespect you or anything like that. I know you may not like what I gotta say, but I just have to say it."

My father looked at me and twisted his lips and walked away from me. I followed right behind him.

"Daddy, you are so selfish, all you think about is yourself. Since I was small all you thought about was yourself. You had these nannies raising me because you didn't have time for me. Before Mommy was even in the ground you was running behind other women. You and I both know that all you care about is you and your ladies."

My father went into the den and slammed the door in my face. I didn't let it deter me. I just kept on venting through closed French glass doors.

"If you broke, then blame that on yourself. You spent money on nannies when you didn't have to.

Nannies that did nothing but fuck my head up! But you don't know nothing about that, do you? You spent money flying all over the world with women and blowing money in casinos and partying and living good and now you want me to bail you out? Well, why the hell didn't you bail me out four or five years ago instead of just shipping me off to Aunt Tanisha's? That would have cost you nothing but time. *Time! Time!*"

I paused for a minute and waited for my father to respond, but he didn't.

"Are you that much of a coward that you can't even talk to me now? What happened to the tears when you found out that I got raped? Was that real or was that just crocodile tears? Daddy, you know what?" I just shook my head and right there I started crying. Inside I was just hoping that my father would say something. I wanted him to say anything. I especially wanted him to open the door and tell me how wrong I was and to hold me and tell me that he loved me and that he was sorry that I felt that way about him. But guess what? He never opened the door.

So through my tears, I continued.

"It was nice having you around the house these past couple of days, and it was nice the way you showed all that concern for me at the police precinct and all of that. But Daddy, I'm no dummy. I thought it was genuine. But the tears, they were crocodile tears. You hanging around and seeming all concerned, that was just an act to get money up outta me."

I didn't want to believe what I was saying, and if my father had just opened the door and attempted to convince me otherwise, I would have given him all the money I had.

What shocked me, though, was that when he did finally open the door, he stood and looked at the tears falling from my eyes. With this look of anger in his face he calmly said, "Shayla, let me explain something to you. You got that money, and it's yours and I'm not gonna beg you for it. But so I don't have to kill you, this is what I want you to do. I want you to take two weeks, and in those two weeks you take a stash of money, find yourself a place, and you move the hell out of my house! You understand me?"

I shook my head. I don't know why I hadn't seen it coming but here it was again, my father was kicking me to the curb once again.

Rage and anger were surging through my body and I just couldn't take it. I started screaming like I was a deranged madwoman.

"I hate you! I fucking hate you! How could you be so goddamn cold?" I screamed and started to attack my father. In the process I knocked down a lamp and some pictures that were in the den.

"You want the money? Okay, I'll give you the fucking money!" I screamed as I hyperventilated and punched on my father. The blows were having no effect on him but I was letting out years of pent-up anger and frustration.

My father finally wrestled control of me. He threw me on the sofa and he held me there and I couldn't move.

"You done?" he asked me.

I looked up at him and I just wanted to spit in his face. I squirmed and tried to loose myself of his grip.

"I said, are you done?"

"Daddy, get off of me!"

"I'll get off of you, but let me just tell you this. Before you ever accuse me of having crocodile tears, you better check your goddamn self. You talk about me being selfish. Okay, I'm human. Maybe I am selfish. But I'm honest and what you need to do, Shayla, is get honest with yourself. Be honest and admit that you ain't nothing but a fast-ass whore!"

When my father said that I almost blacked out from anger. I started kicking him and trying my best to crush his balls and get free of his grip.

"You know and I know that you ain't get raped that night. I backed your ass like a father should back his daughter, even though I knew you was lying. I guess that was me being selfish too, right? Yet you gonna sit here and accuse me of having crocodile tears?"

My father finally loosened his grip on me and shoved me deeper into the sofa and he prepared to get up.

"I want you outta here in two weeks," he reiterated.

If I had a knife or a gun on me, at that point I would have killed my father right there on the spot.

I was enraged. I reached back in my throat as far as I could reach. I hocked up the most spit that I could muster up, let it go with as much force as I could derive from my body and hurled it right at my father's face.

The spit landed right in my father's eye. I got total satisfaction out of seeing the spit land on his face and in his eye. That momentary satisfaction would never be able to make up for the irreparable damage that my father's stinging words and actions had caused me.

All throughout my life he had managed to penetrate my soul and wound me deeper than humanly imaginable. As I seethed in anger, I had to remind myself that he was just being consistent with who he had been throughout my entire life.

One thing was for sure and that was that I hated his guts. He didn't have to worry about me leaving in two weeks. I knew that I would be outta there and on my own in more like two days! I didn't know if he was really in danger of losing the house and I really didn't care because in all likelihood he wasn't in as bad shape as he had made it out to be.

Unfortunately, though, I also had a strong feeling that I was about to relapse into my old promiscuous ways.

Chapter Twenty

New Friends

Tara and I did end up hooking up with each other later that night. In fact, Tara, myself, and three of her stripper friends ended up going to this club called Octagon in Manhattan. One thing is for sure and that's that partying with money is a whole lot more fun than partying without it.

Although Tara and I both had money, I was the one who did most of the spending. I splurged and bought not one, but two bottles of Moët for all of us who were partying that night. I ended up buying a total of ten bottles!

My lavish spending and all the bottles of bubbly instantly attracted attention in our direction. In no time we had a crowd of people in the lounge area where we were partying in.

I soon found myself dancing with white guys, Colombian guys, Spanish guys, black guys, and even some chicks danced with me. Before I knew it, I was twisted and drunk as hell.

"Yo, Tara. *Gggürrrrl* I love you girl," I screamed into her ear over the loud music with slurred speech.

Tara snatched me up and hugged me. Then the two of us began dancing with each other and grinding on each other to a Shabba Ranks songs.

"Don't be grinding on me like that," I playfully yelled into Tara's ear.

"Yo, hand me my bottle of Mo."

One of her friends quickly grabbed Tara's bottle and my bottle.

"We gotta toast to your birthday," Tara screamed out to me.

"You know that's right," I said as I raised my bottle up and touched Tara's.

We both took a swig from our bottles. When I was done, I shouted to her, "Yo, you look extra sexy tonight."

"Money will do that to you," Tara shot back at me as she started laughing.

Then without warning or anything, something just came over me. I pulled Tara close to me with my free hand. The bottle of Moet was in my other hand and I started tongue kissing her right there on the dance floor. Tara was caught off guard but she started to kiss me back.

"Oh, sookey-sookey now," one of Tara's friends said to us as she intervened and brought our lustful lesbian kiss to an end.

The liquor had me tore down. I was in such a good mood I simply moved on and started dancing with some random guy as the DJ switched up the music and threw on Naughty by Nature's song "O.P.P."

The crowd and everybody on the dance floor went crazy when that song came on. The funny thing is that after that song went off I literally don't remember much of anything else that happened because I was just so damn drunk.

The next thing that I do remember is that I was getting out of the passenger side of my car and then getting into an elevator with Tara and one of her friends who had been at Octagon with us. Her friend's name was Juanita. We must have been at Juanita's house but I couldn't say with certainty just where the hell I was at.

From the time that the elevator doors opened up to let us out I barely remember much that happened after that. What I do know is that somehow at like 7:00 that next morning I woke up butt-ass naked. Not only that but I found myself in a king-sized bed with Tara and Juanita. We were all butt-ass naked with some sex toys lying right next to the bed.

I sat up on the bed trying to figure out just where the hell I was and more importantly, what the fuck had I done.

I couldn't sit up for too long because I felt sick as a dog and I wanted to lay right back down. Before I could fully lay back down I looked across the room and saw some dude sleeping in a folding chair and all he had on was his boxers.

What the fuck? Who in the hell is that? I asked myself as I lay back down on the bed and attempted to go back to sleep. I decided to try and just sort everything out later on after fully waking up.

I eventually did wake up at about noon. When I woke up, Tara and Juanita woke up right after me.

"You all right?" Tara asked me as she got outta the bed and attempted to put on some clothes.

"Nah, my head is killing me and my stomach feels real queasy," I said to her as I laid my ass right back down. I still had no clue as to what borough I was in or anything relevant of that nature.

I tapped Tara and got her attention and then I whispered, "Yo, where in the hell am I at? And who the hell is he?" I said while pointing in the direction of the guy who was still asleep in his boxers.

Juanita and Tara both looked at each other and they both burst out laughing at the same time.

"You joking, right?" Juanita asked me.

I gave her this look as if to say, *does it look like I'm joking.*

"Shayla, you was straight wildin'-out last night," Tara said to me.

At that point the guy who was asleep in the chair woke up and he also looked like he was trying to figure out where in the hell he was.

"What up what up?" the guy said.

We all just looked at him without saying a word.

"Yo Juanita, where's your bathroom at?" he asked as he got up and made his way outta the bedroom and into the hallway.

By that question I was able to determine that we were at Juanita's house, but I still needed to know just what I had done the night before.

"Shayla, I gotta get this nigga up outta my crib!" Juanita whispered to me.

"And?" I said as I finally mustered up the strength to get out of the bed and stand up.

"And he's here for you! So tell me what you want me to do with his ass!"

"What are you talking about?"

Juanita and Tara both doubled over and were laughing and covering their mouths to mask the noise.

"Shayla, you fucked that nigga last night, you do know that, don't you?" Juanita managed to say to me through her laughter.

"You have got to be joking! That short little nigga! I don't even know him!"

"Juanita, just round up his shit and tell him he's got to go," Tara said as she began scooping up the guy's clothes and shoes while also laughing her ass off.

Juanita put on a robe. She headed down the hall and to her bathroom. After she knocked on the bathroom door all I heard was, "Oh hell nawh! Okay look you has definitely gots to get your black ass up outta here!"

Tara started to tell me something about the night before but she was quickly summoned by Juanita to come to the bathroom.

"Tara, bring that nigga's clothes over here so he can bounce," Juanita yelled. "Do you believe that this nigga was brushing his teeth with my goddamn toothbrush?"

"Yo, you ain't even gotta come outta your face like that. I'm saying, I ain't even here for yo ass anyway," the short guy hollered at Juanita.

"Shayla, you better come speak to this dude," Juanita screamed at me.

I quickly threw on the clothes that I had worn to the club and I scrambled and made it to the entrance of the bathroom.

"Shayla, I'm outta here, but let me get your number before I bounce," the guy said to me.

I had the most confused look on my face.

"Yo, I don't even know who the hell you are," I said to the guy. "Who are you?"

Juanita and Tara tried to hold back their laughter but they couldn't.

"Whateva man! Y'all chicks is really on some other shit," the guy said as he finished putting on his clothes.

Juanita walked to the door and held it open for the guy. He took the hint and made his way out of the apartment before he could fully put on his shoes.

Juanita slammed the door behind the guy and it almost hit him in the ass. Tara literally fell on the floor in laughter and she couldn't stop laughing.

"Do you believe that motherfucker? Just gonna up and use my toothbrush. What the hell is that? That's some ol' nasty-ass shit."

"And you see them little ol' short stubby legs on that nigga?" Tara said as she continued to hold her stomach from laughing.

Finally, after a few minutes her and Juanita got ahold of themselves and were in control of their laughter. They had calmed down and were able to tell me all of the craziness that I had did the night before.

In summary I had wigged out and wild out big-time.

They told me how I had started tossing hundred-dollar bills into the air and screaming that I was rich. More specifically, I was hollering, "I'm rich bitch!"

They told me how I had all kinds of men coming on to me and that I asked Juanita and Tara if they'd dare me to scoop the short dude who had just left Juanita's house. I had done all kinds of things that I didn't remember, like cursing out the car window at every police car that we saw on the street. Having Juanita pull to the side of the road so that I could piss in the street like a dude.

I couldn't believe any of what they were telling me. At the same time I knew that they were telling the truth. I knew that because I had allowed myself to get drunker than I had ever been simply because I had wanted to be as numb as never before. It was like I wanted to escape being me and alcohol provided that escape for me. It helped mask the pain that I was feeling.

The funny thing was that after my drunkenness and my hangover had worn off, I felt more pain than I had felt prior to my getting drunk the night before. I guess that my pain was compounded by the fact that when reality set in, I realized that I had blown five thousand dollars in one night. I had also let my mom down by fucking some short, stubby nigga that I didn't even know and having a lesbian orgy with Juanita and Tara. The sad part was that I had gotten to such a low level that I was having sex with strange, random people and not even remembering any of it a few hours later.

I knew that with money I would be able to medicate myself some more. Not to mention that Tara had supplied me with three brand-new friends, Juanita being one of them, who loved to have me around, or so I thought. The truth, as I would later find out, is that when you have money everybody is willing to be your friend. Unfortunately for me, I didn't realize until thousands of blown dollars later that Tara, Juanita, mat all.

Three and a half months down the road, when my bank account began to really dwindle to the frighteningly low amount of 20,000 dollars and I pulled back on the splurging, partying, and sponsoring Caribbean and Mexican vacations, Juanita, Tara, and the crew did me like everyone else in my lifetime had done me.

Yup, my so-called new friends dropped me like a bad habit after using me and abusing me.
But it was a'ight though. I would be a'ight.
At least I hoped I would be.

Chapter Twenty-one

Ms. Boswell

On New Year's eve 1991 I found myself alone in my one thousand dollar a month two bedroom apartment, which was located just off of Queens Boulevard in the Rego Park section of Queens. Dick Clark was on TV preparing to ring in the New Year and I was on my living room sofa trying to drink myself into a coma.

I felt more depressed than I had ever been. And I had good reason to feel depressed. Yeah, granted, for the past couple of months I had been driving around in a brand-new Mercedes Benz 190E, a car which I had paid for with twenty thousand dollars in cash. For one thousand dollars a month I was subletting a gorgeous duplex two-bedroom condo with a lobby that had a twenty four hour a day doorman. My apartment was fully furnished with high-end furniture that I had also paid for in full with cash. My walk-in closets were all filled with racks and racks of shoes and clothes from all of the top-name designers. Even the walls in my apartment held pictures of me and Tara from the four Caribbean vacations that we had taken together.

Despite all of those material things that I had to make me feel comfortable, I was still feeling lonely as hell and deeply depressed. Tara and my so-called crew of friends acted so shady toward me after the money dried up that I practically stopped speaking to them. In fact, aside from calling Tara to check in on her every now and then, I really had no one else that I would speak to or deal with. No female friends and no male friends or boyfriends. My father had all but disowned me and he stopped speaking to me after I wouldn't loan him that money. Although I had given him my new phone number and my new address, he never called me nor did he come by to see my new place. What hurt me the most was that he didn't even call me to check on how things were progressing with my whole rape ordeal.

When the blood test of the rape suspect Antonio Reid had come back from the lab and it confirmed that his blood type had matched that of the semen stain that was found on my clothes, I thought for sure that I would hear from my father. But I never heard from him. Actually, I had this little dreamy fantasy that after my father had found out that the rapist's blood type matched the semen stain that he would call me and apologize for insinuating and saying that I hadn't been raped. Unfortunately, that was just a fantasy because my father never called.

The assistant district attorney had me come into her office a week after the blood type was confirmed as a match. What she explained to me was that not only did the blood type match but that Antonio Reid had one of the most rare blood types in the world. He had an AB blood type.

I can still hear the joy in her voice and the elation on her face as she grabbed me and hugged me and said, "Shayla, do you know what this means? This means we're gonna nail this bastard and send him away for more than twenty years! Only four percent of the population has that blood type. Four percent, that's it—just one in every ten thousand people have that rare of a blood type. So for you and Tara to pick him out of a lineup and for his blood type to match, combined with the fact that he admittedly was in Manhattan at the time the rape occurred, and he has a violent past—Shayla, you're gonna get the justice that is due you. It's open-and-shut."

Man, when I left the district attorney's office that day I was so elated and felt so vindicated that I instinctively called my father. I had to share the news with him. I called him repeatedly at his house and at his girlfriend's house and I never got anyone to pick up the phone. I left numerous messages telling him the good news about the certainty of the rapist based on the odds of his rare blood type. Still I got no answer from my pops.

The pain I felt from feeling like my dad had scorned me was what sent me over the edge as far as splurging and spending. I guess I was trying to buy myself friends and relationships of substance so I shelled out thousands and thousands. After it was all said and done, when Dick Clark announced that it was now 1992, I was feeling empty.

About twenty minutes after the new year had rung in I rushed to my bathroom because I had to throw up. All the liquor that I had been drinking was ready to come out and I soon found myself worshiping the porcelain god, better known as the toilet bowl.

I felt horrible. With spit hanging from my mouth and chunks of regurgitated food on my clothes I plopped my face on the floor and just lay there stretched out on the cold bathroom floor feeling depressed. A thought flashed threw my mind that told me to get up and get a razor blade and slit both of my wrists. I probably would have carried that out but I didn't have the wits or the energy to get up and make it to my room to get a razor blade so I just laid there.

"God, please just help me," I said very softly. "Please God, help me," I said again as tears started to form in my eyes.

I thought about my mom and how I wanted to make her proud of me. Then, as I laid there it was like I could hear this voice in my head that kept telling me to call Ms. Boswell. The voice kept saying it over and over and over again. It was like the voice was getting louder and louder. *Get up and call her right now and tell her everything*, the voice said.

I was confused, dazed, drunk, sick, and an overall hot mess. But on my hands and knees I still managed to crawl back to my living room. I found my pocketbook and I retrieved Ms. Boswell's card.

It read: *Andrea Boswell, Manhattan District Attorney*.

It also had all of her office contact info on the front of the card, and on the back of the card was Ms. Boswell's cell phone number and her home telephone number, which she had handwritten specifically for me to have.

See, she had recently taken over for the previous Manhattan district attorney. Ms. Boswell was not the district attorney on the night I had been raped. In fact, she had taken over as the district attorney about two weeks prior to the new year.

What had impressed me about her was that she was a young black woman who seemed to have it all. Probably because she was a black woman, I was able to identify with her. More than just her being black, I was able to connect with Ms. Boswell because she gave off this radiant, powerful energy that I wanted to possess. She was gorgeous and she reminded me a lot of the former Miss America Vanessa Williams. Ms. Bowell had this way about her that whenever I was in her presence or spoke to her she would make me feel like I was the most important person in the world and the only thing that mattered to her at the moment.

Out of the genuine and pure kindness of her heart she had called me when she took over as district attorney and invited me down to her office so she could meet me and talk to me and, as she put it, get to know me. Even after that initial meeting she had invited me back to her office so that she and I could go out to lunch together, her treat.

At that lunch I remember asking her, "Ms. Boswell, out of all the cases that your office is handling, why did you choose to call me and treat me to lunch and all of that? You do this with everybody?"

Ms. Boswell cracked a smile and she looked at me.

"First off, you gotta stop calling me Ms. Boswell. You're making me feel old. I'm only thirty-seven. Jeez, Call me Andrea, okay?" she said in a joking way.

I smiled and nodded my head.

"Honestly, God put it on my heart to call you. I mean, I had heard about your case prior to me taking over as the district attorney. When I came in I wanted to familiarize myself with all of the cases and you just became a priority to me."

"But why?"

She smiled again.

"Because, I wanted to see if I would see some of me in you."

"What?" I asked as she had confused the heck outta me.

"See, when I was young like you are, eighteen, nineteen, twenty years old, you couldn't have called anyone who knew me and convinced them otherwise that I wasn't gonna end up with a bunch of kids by a bunch of different men, be on welfare, and probably strung out on drugs if I didn't get killed or ended up in jail first."

"Really?" I said as I took a sip of my Sprite.

"Really."

I looked at Ms. Boswell and saw how stunningly beautiful she was. I told her that she looked like what every black woman probably strives to look like.

She smiled and then she told me, "It wasn't always like this."

She went on to tell me that she could sense in my spirit that she and I were similar in many ways and that she wouldn't be able to confirm that until I allowed her to get to know me.

I just looked at her and didn't say anything.

"But, you know what? You probably won't allow me, or anyone else for that matter, to get to really know you because you don't trust anyone."

I sipped on my Sprite again and I didn't say anything. Nor did Ms. Boswell force me to say anything.

"Shayla, I'm old enough to be your mom, I know that. In fact, I have a son and a daughter who are twenty and twenty-one. But I still want to be your friend if that's okay."

I shook my head and put a forkful of food into my mouth and I smiled.

"Why?" I asked her through my food-filled smile.

She simply started to open up about herself and she began telling me how she had gotten pregnant at sixteen and then again at seventeen. She had dropped out of high school and she was living so wild and misguided that the state took her kids from her when they were babies because she was endangering their welfare. She went on to tell me how she had had numerous abortions and had experimented with drugs and sex before getting hooked on drugs and all kinds of stuff that I would have never believed.

At one point I wanted to just sit there with my mouth wide open and stare at her in amazement.

"So how did you become a district attorney if you been through all of that?"

"I straightened myself out and I worked my ass off," Ms. Boswell said.

She then went on to explain that the social worker who had taken her kids away from her had practically stalked her in order to befriend her. She said that the social worker saw something in her that had substance and quality and she was determined to be a part of Ms. Boswell's life until she could see and value that substance and quality.

"I owe everything to that social worker and to God. There were a whole lot of things in between that I had to do in order to develop the discipline to become a better me. But the thing that I know is that I wouldn't have been able to get to where I'm at if I didn't have someone who believed in me enough to not give up on me."

"Wow," I replied.

We continued to talk and eat and before we were ready to leave she said, "Shayla, you know what's funny? I send people to prison every day but nine out of ten times, those people who I send to prison are already in prison."

"What do you mean?"

"What I mean is that, all prisons are not made of bars of steel and concrete. The biggest prisons are the prisons of our minds. If people could just escape or free themselves from that prison that is in their minds then they would more than likely never end up in jail in the first place. The physical jails and prisons just become an extension and a continuation of what they were already experiencing mentally."

I looked at Ms. Boswell in amazement. It was like she was some kind of goddess or something with all of this knowledge, perception, and deep insight.

"Until I freed myself from that mental prison that I was in, my life didn't change and it wouldn't have changed. I didn't get out of that prison until I started opening up and letting that social worker really get to know me. She knew me like I know you, but she didn't know Andrea just like I don't know Shayla."

I sighed and I looked at her but I didn't say anything. What I was thinking was that I don't let anyone get to know me because I don't wanna be vulnerable to anyone.

That was when she interrupted my thoughts, took out her card, scribbled down her cell phone number and her home phone number, and told me to call her at anytime and for anything.

So there I was on the night that the New Year had rung in. I was in a complete state of hot-messness and I found myself on my hands and knees dialing Ms. Boswell's cell phone number.

"District Attorney Boswell speaking," she answered after three rings.

"Hello," I softly spoke into the phone.

"Yes, this is Ms. Boswell, who's speaking?"

"Ms. Boswell, this is Shayla."

"Hey Shayla. Happy New Year, girl," she spoke with a perky voice that had switched from businesslike to a friendly tone.

"I'm sorry to bother you on New Year's eve and all that. But I really need to speak to you."

Right after saying that, I coughed and threw up again right there on my living room floor.

"Shayla. Hello? Shayla, you okay?"

I paused and wiped my mouth and I told her that I wasn't okay and that I was feeing depressed and had had too much to drink.

"Where are you?"

"I'm at home."

"Are you alone?"

"Yeah. I called you 'cause I just feel like killing myself," I said as tears began to well up in my eyes.

"Shayla, what's wrong, sweetie?"

"Everything is wrong," I replied.

"Listen, give me your address," she stated to me.

I softly spoke my address into the phone. Ms. Boswell took it down and she told me that she was gonna leave the function that she was at and come over to see me. She wanted me to stay on the phone with her until she got there.

"You don't have to do that," I said.

"Shayla, I know that, but I want to do it."

When she said that, I could hear a slight sniffle sound as if she was crying.

"You gonna come now?" I asked.

"Yes, I'm on my way. Listen, nothing is that bad. It may appear that way, but trust me, it's not. I want you to remember what I'm gonna say," she said. I could tell that she was clearly crying at this point. She continued on: "Killing yourself is just a horrible long-term solution to a short-term problem and *all* problems can be solved, baby."

I paused and didn't say anything. I reached for my remote control and I turned off the television because I was tired of seeing happy white people celebrating the New Year.

"Can you promise me something?" I asked as I too began to cry.

"Anything, what is it?" Ms. Boswell quickly said.

"If I tell you some stuff . . . it's not good stuff, though. Can you promise me that you won't stop speaking to me?"

"Shayla, listen to me, sweetie—"

I cut her off while she was talking and through hyperventilating-type of crying, I added, "I mean, like 'cause with your job and all, you may not be able to speak to me anymore."

"Baby, there is nothing—and I mean nothing—that you could tell me that would make me stop speaking to you. I'll always tell you the truth and you may not like the truth, but I will always be your friend. Remember, Shayla, I told you the worst about me, and I can tell you more about me that would really make your head spin, and yet you still called me tonight, right? You did that because we're friends. Friends are only true friends when they know the worst about you and they still choose to be your friend."

"Okay," I said to her.

She continued to talk to me as she drove in her Acura Legend from Harlem toward Queens.

I felt physically horrible from the liquor but mentally I felt even worse. One thing was for sure and that was that I was more than ready to let myself out of that mental prison that I was in.

Chapter Twenty-two

Mom

Ms. Boswell got to my apartment in about a half an hour.

"Hey sweetie," she said to me when I opened the door.

"Hey," I replied. I was still feeling horrible but her presence had made me start to feel a little bit better.

"Ms. Boswell, I'm sorry that I got you here on New Year's eve like this."

"Andrea. Shayla, my name is Andrea and that's what I want you to call me. Okay?"

Andrea walked up to me and she attempted to give me a hug but I stopped her because of my filthy, vomit-stained shirt.

"Girl, you better give me a hug!" Andrea said as she grabbed me and just held me close to her.

I felt like a little baby and I just wanted to melt in her arms. What's funny is that while she held me she didn't say a word. Immediately my mind started to wonder just what was Andrea's true intentions. *Oh my God, Ms. Boswell is a lesbian!* I thought. *She came over here so she could try and get with me sexually.*

I wanted to pull back from her, but truth be told, had she made a sexual pass at me and tried to take it somewhere sexually, I know that I would have went along with it. That's just how twisted and confused my mind was.

After about two minutes or so Andrea loosened her hug and she told me that what she wanted me to do was to go take a shower and clean myself up and to go to sleep.

"Go to sleep?" I asked.

"Yup. That's what you need right now. I want you to go to sleep and sleep off what you drank and let your body reenergize itself."

"So you're gonna leave?" I asked with a disappointed tone.

"No. What I'm gonna do, if it's okay with you, is I'm gonna clean up that mess over there that you made, I'm gonna fall asleep right there on that sofa and when we wake up I'm gonna chill with you and we'll hang out and talk."

I frowned and tilted my head while I looked at her.

"Are you for real?"

"Yes, I'm for real."

The way that Andrea said that she was gonna chill with me was a perfect example of just why I connected with her and why I was so fascinated with her. She was this highly educated, powerful woman, yet she talked the way I talked and used words like *gonna* and *chill*, and that helped me relate to her.

So I went along with Andrea's plan and I did as she said. I took a nice, hot shower and went straight to my bed. My bed had never felt so good.

By the time ten o'clock that next morning rolled in, I opened my eyes and I continued to lay in my bed. My stomach was still a little queasy but my headache had disappeared. I listened and I could hear the sound of the TV coming from the living room. I could tell that Andrea was still there because it sounded as if she was changing channels.

Although I wanted to get up, I was still not feeling at my best so I closed my eyes and went back to sleep. Finally, at around one o'clock I fully woke up and got out of my bed. I put on my robe and I walked to the living room and greeted Andrea.

"Happy New Year," I said with a smile plastered across my face.

"Happy New Year to you too. Did you sleep good?"

"Definitely, and I feel a whole lot better too."

Andrea smiled as she got up and walked to my kitchen. I followed behind her.

"You're good, 'cause back in the days I would have to sleep until five o'clock in the evening in order to recover from my hangovers."

"Really?" I smiled and said as I sat at my kitchen table.

Andrea nodded and she informed me that she was gonna cook us some pancakes.

"So talk to me," she said. "Tell me anything. Matter of fact, just tell me the first thing that comes to your mind. Don't worry about what I'll think."

I paused for a moment and then I almost spit out my orange juice because I started laughing.

"What's so funny?" Andrea asked.

"You said to tell you anything, right?"

Andrea looked at me and nodded.

"Okay, well, honestly, what's running through my head right now—and the same thought popped into my head last night before I went to sleep. I just can't help it but something keeps saying to me that you're a lesbian and you're only being this nice to me and coming over here like you did and all of that because you wanna get with me sexually."

Andrea looked at me and she started to laugh.

"Okay. Okay. That's good. It's funny and not true but it's good that you told me that. You're being honest and I like that."

I was getting ready to say something else but Andrea cut me off and she said, "But you don't have to worry about that because trust me, I'm strictly-dickly."

We both fell out laughing after she said that.

Andrea then started to pour the pancake batter into the skillet and she said to me, "So if you don't mind me asking, have you been with a woman before?"

Instantly my heart started racing with anxiety. I wasn't exactly sure how I should answer her. I paused and in my mind I was like, what the hell, just answer the damn question truthfully.

"Yeah," I said and then I sort of mentally braced myself to get attacked and judged by her.

"I bet you never told anybody that, right?"

"No," I said with a nervous smile. My anxiety was beginning to lighten.

"Girl, it's okay," Andrea said in response to my nervous smile.

Andrea flipped the pancakes and then there was more silence as she checked on the bacon that she was frying.

My heart really started to race and I got really nervous and anxious as I contemplated should I tell her about Joyce, my nanny from back in the days, who had introduced me to sex.

I buried my hands into my face and pressed my hands against my face as if I was trying to literally bury my face into my hands. I visibly exhaled air from my lungs before I started to speak.

"You know something that I never, ever told anybody?" I said to her. I felt like crying from the thought of just thinking that I was about to divulge information that I had held inside for more than nine years.

"What's that?"

"Well, when I was young, like nine years old, we had this live-in nanny named Joyce. Joyce was the first person who introduced me to sex and I had my first sexual experience with a woman."

Andrea didn't say anything and her silence made me more nervous and more anxious so I just began to speak before she had a chance to speak up and condemn me.

"Yeah, she introduced me to porno movies and vibrators and all of that. She even let her boyfriends have sex with me."

"Wow, Shayla! You never said anything to anyone about this? Not even your dad?"

I shook my head from side to side and I didn't say anything.

"Shayla, do you know what incest is?"

I shook my head no.

Andrea then went on to explain to me what it was and she opened up and told me how her own father had sexually molested her starting when she was twelve years old.

"So that's how I got introduced to sex."

The kitchen got really quiet as the food was ready and Andrea placed everything on the table so that we could start eating.

The next thing I know is that it was six o'clock in the evening. I was still in my robe and Andrea and I were still at the kitchen table talking. Five hours had gone by but in those five hours I had became an open book and I unlocked the doors to the mental prison that I had been in.

I told Andrea everything about me—everything.

I told her all about my dad, the nannies, my Aunt Tanisha, the underground sex parties, the abortions, my cousin raping me, my independent one-girl call-girl service, the drinking, the masturbating, my porno collection and sex toy collection, Pink Chocolate, the two hundred and some odd thousand dollars that I had blown, and my fake friends and how I allowed them to use me. All throughout my talking I was able to maintain my composure, but when I began to talk about my mom, I just couldn't control my emotions.

I had saved talking about her 'til toward the end of the conversation that we were having because I knew that too many raw emotions would come out. I told Andrea about how my mom had came back to visit me one night, and after I said that, my tears just started falling and they wouldn't stop.

"Andrea, I just feel like everything that happened to me in my life wouldn't have happened to me if my mom had been with me. I can't help it, but I get so angry at her and at God for her not being there for me," I said through my tears.

Andrea hugged me.

"I understand, baby. It's not fair, it's not right, and it hurts. It's painful and I know that it hurts so much because you love your mom dearly."

I nodded my head up and down.

"I do. But it's like I just can't figure out why I had to be the one to grow up without a mom. I hated that all my life and I resent it even to this day!"

"Shayla, it's not fair. You deserved to have your mom with you while you grew up. And you have a right to be angry. But you know something? Your mom loved you and she still loves you more than you would ever know. It's easy to get angry at her but even through your anger I want you to think about this. Number one, think about how many people lose loved ones who weren't smart enough to take out an insurance policy on themselves. That didn't happen with your mom because she loved you enough to think about your well-being in the event of her untimely absence. Number two, think about how profound it was for your mom to look ahead and structure the insurance payments the way she did. She let you get half of your money when you turned eighteen and she is letting you get the other half at twenty-one. I bet that she did that because she knew that even if she wasn't around that you would still have to be your own person. You would have to fall on your own and get back up and face life as your own individual self with the cards that life dealt you. Your mom knew that you probably wouldn't be prepared to have that kind of money at that age. And you know what? It's okay that you weren't ready for that kind of money because you're human and life goes on. But guess what, when you get your next check at twenty-one, think about how much wiser you're gonna be with that money and how it will enhance your life instead of hindering it. And you have only your mom to thank for that."

I wiped my tears and I thought about what Andrea had said and how right she was.

"All of those things that your mom told you when she visited you . . . girl, your mom may not be with you physically but trust me, she is with you every day. Her spirit is still alive and the best thing is that you can talk to her 24–7 and get advice and answers from her by just listening to your spirit, because part of her will forever be in you."

"You're right," I said.

I knew that this conversation that Andrea and I were having would forever change me. I would have to later go back and reflect on all of the things that she said to me, but inside I felt very funny because I knew that there was still something that I was holding back.

Andrea and I were both silent until I broke the silence.

"Andrea, I appreciate you being here for me like this. You just don't know what it means. But . . . um . . . I know you're gonna be upset with me with what I'm about to tell you. And if you are and if you decide to put distance between us, I'll understand and I'll still be grateful for you."

"Girl, what nonsense are you talking?" Andrea asked me.

I shook my head and I just went for it. "Well, with my rape and all. Remember how I told you I was working at the Pink Chocolate strip club as a bartender?"

"Yeah."

I sighed and said, "Well, the night that I got raped, what really happened was these guys had paid me three hundred dollars to have sex with both of them and I took the money but I changed my mind. Instead of giving them the money back I got nervous and scared and I tried to just leave the club and bounce on them without giving them their money back. But they was hip to me and they caught me at my car and put me in their truck and drove off with me and raped me."

Andrea was silent in her thoughts. I could just tell that she was heated and getting ready to let me have it.

She blew air out of her lungs and then she calmly asked me, "so you did get raped, though, right?"

"Yes, without a doubt. I would tell you now if I was lying. The thing was, I just lied to the cops because I didn't want anyone to know that I had been coming from Pink Chocolate, because then no one would have believed me and aside from that everyone would have just labeled me as a ho. Plus, I was too young to have been working in there and that would have brought on all kinds of heat for the strip club, which would have made things worse for me in the long run."

"So, what about Tara's story and her picking out the same suspect that you did?"

I told Andrea how I had paid Tara the fifteen thousand dollars and how we got our story together in order to not say anything that would conflict.

Andrea bit on her bottom lip. She didn't look me in my face. She just sat and thought to herself. I remained silent.

"Tell me this. The guy that you picked out of the mug shots and out of the lineup, are you certain without a shadow of a doubt that that is the guy who raped you?"

"Absolutely," I said without hesitation. I went on to tell Andrea how the guy who raped me was the same guy from years ago who had paid me at the underground sex party, but he hadn't sexed me and he felt like I was playing him for a second time in the same way.

"Shayla, are you sure for sure that he's the guy?"

"Andrea, I am positive. I wouldn't lie about that and I would definitely tell you now if I was lying."

"Okay, I appreciate your honesty," Andrea said as she blew out a mountain of air from her lungs before continuing on.

"Now, here's the thing. We can still get a conviction but it's gonna be tough because now your credibility is gonna be questioned to no end. The thing is that the suspect was still in Manhattan on the night that you were raped and the chances on his rare blood type matching the semen stain is such a slam-dunk that it should be enough to overcome the credibility thing. I just can't guarantee it because the jury may think if you lied about that, then you could be lying about the whole thing."

"Well, why don't we just not say anything?" I asked.

"Can't do that," Andrea said while shaking her head. "Always tell the truth no matter what. Shayla, most of your life you have been lying either directly or indirectly to keep your past a secret. I was the same way, but if you wanna live life on another level and live life to the fullest, you gotta tell the truth all the time no matter what."

Andrea then went on to explain that the biggest hurdle would be overcoming the grand jury testimonies that Tara and I had given because it would be considered perjury and that is a crime.

She assured me that she would be able to have us state the truth and still get around the perjury issue. She just felt that with the trial only eight months away that it would be better to get things out in the open now as opposed to later.

From that point on, as Andrea and I talked, I could tell that her mind wasn't as focused on me. It was like the wheels in her head were turning and probably thinking about my rape case.

However, I felt safe that I wouldn't lose Andrea as a friend. In fact, before she left my apartment, as she was standing in my doorway and ready to go, she cemented in my mind that she was true and genuine and would be there for me with no ulterior motive.

"Shayla, you know why that rape occurred?"

I was kind of confused by what she was asking me.

"My rape?"

"Yes."

"I don't know what you mean."

"Well, what I'm trying to say is that I believe in my heart that the reason that you were raped was so that our paths could cross and I could be there for you."

"You really think so?" I said. I was feeling so esteemed, like I really mattered to her. I felt my eyes beginning to water up.

I reached out and just hugged her.

"Thank you, Andrea," I said as tears rolled down my cheeks.

It was now about seven-thirty and although Andrea had been at my house for hours, it felt like time had flown by. I didn't want her to go.

As I continued to hug her, I said through my tears, "Andrea, would you mind if I call you Mom from now on?"

Andrea pushed back from me slightly so that she could look at me and she had the biggest smile on her face.

"Of course you can," she said as she wiped away tears from the left side of my face.

"But only if you make me some small promises."

"Anything," I said.

"Promise me that you're gonna learn to forgive and let go. And where only God can provide justice, you will learn to still forgive and let go and be cool with that."

"Deal," I replied.

"And there's gonna come a time when someone crosses your path and they're gonna need you to be there for them and help them unconditionally like I want to do for you. Just promise me that if and when that happens that you'll not only be alert to their situation and their needs, but you'll respond and do whatever it takes to make a difference in their life."

I nodded my head up and down and said, "*Mom*, you ain't say nothing but a word. Consider it done."

With that, Andrea and I embraced one more time before she departed. I had such euphoria running through my body that I went back into my apartment, turned on my radio and just blasted music. As the music blasted I danced around like an absolute fool. I had the biggest and best party that I had ever had. I was the only person at the party, but it was all good. I didn't need to party with anyone but myself.

I danced and celebrated my new freedom. I had just been released from that mental prison that I had been in for years. And man, there is no other feeling in the world that can compare to freedom.

I was ready to move into a new phase of my life. I couldn't wait because now I had one of the baddest, smartest, prettiest moms to help me navigate my way through life.

Part III

The Adult Years

Chapter Twenty-three

The Witness Stand

Between the first of the year and August of 1992 a lot had transpired in my life. Aside from preparing me for my rape trial, Andrea and I had continued to develop a strong bond and she treated me as if I really was her daughter. I hung out a lot with her biological daughter and for the first time in my life I started to see what genuine friendship was all about.

Also during that time Andrea had pulled some strings for me to get a trainee position at a brokerage firm on Wall Street. I had been working at the brokerage firm since February 1992. I loved every minute of it and I loved the money that I made while working there.

In the midst of everything she continually urged and encouraged me to go to college. With her urging and my knowing that going to college would also please my real mom, I applied to about ten different colleges. Surprisingly, I was accepted to each and every college that I had applied to. More importantly, I had been accepted to Howard University, which was the school that I desperately wanted to attend.

Although I had many positive things that were happening and my world was finally moving away from all of the dysfunction it had known, I had to deal with the reality of my rape case going to trial, which of course meant that I would have to testify on the witness stand, something that I was not looking forward to doing.

The trial began on the first Monday in August. What was so sad and probably made me feel worse than getting raped was the fact that my father never showed up to the courtroom to support me. I had called him and left messages for him but he never responded to me. I had even unsuccessfully tried to make physical contact with him prior to the start of the trial to let him know that I would be attending Howard University, but I could never catch him at home.

Thankfully, though, my Aunt Tanisha was there for me and she was at the courtroom sitting in the first row day in and day out. She and I would talk before and after proceedings and during breaks. Aunt Tanisha always found a way to say the right things to me at the right times. She was one of my biggest anchors and I needed her more than ever, especially when I took the stand to testify on my own behalf.

However, prior to my testimony, Tara had taken the stand to testify *against* me.

Yeah, Tara really had no choice but to testify against me because the deal that Andrea's office had worked out to the liking of Antonio Reid's lawyer was that Tara would not have to worry about facing any criminal perjury charges so long as she was fully willing to participate as a witness for the defense. I, on the other hand, was able to avoid perjury charges because Andrea had worked it out where in exchange for not prosecuting me on that charge, the charge of aggravated assault would be dropped from the indictment against Antonio Reid.

Well, day one of the trial was spent with opening arguments from the defense and from the prosecution. The witnesses that were called to the witness stand were the cops, detectives, paramedics, and doctors.

But on day two, Tara was the first witness called to the stand. I hadn't spoken to or seen Tara since December of 1991 and it was now August 1992. Tara looked good; she looked like she had slimmed down a bit, but that might have been because of the way that she was dressed. She had on a business suit that made her look like a Goody-Two-Shoes bank teller. She had cut her hair really short and had the Halle Berry short hair look. Tara casually walked to the witness stand. Her signature high heel shoes were notably absent from her feet. She wore a pair of plain black leather flat shoes.

Instinctively I smiled when I saw her and how good she looked. It was instinctive, because I had known her since I was in the ninth grade. Although I had purposely kept away from her in the eight months that preceded the trial, I still had a level of love for her.

After Tara had raised her hand and swore on the Bible to tell the truth and nothing but the truth, she looked square in my direction. I visibly smiled at her and on the inside I was hoping like hell that she would do the right thing by me and help boost my case with her testimony even though she was now a witness for the defense.

Tara seemed to be thinking totally the opposite than what I was thinking, because she rolled her eyes at me and gave me this vicious ice grill.

The defense attorney began asking her questions about me. He started off with real subtle questions like how long had Tara known me and where did we meet. But before long the defense attorney stepped it up with his questions.

"You and Shayla Coleman were pretty close friends at one point, would you say?"

"Yes. We were like best friends," Tara replied.

"Did the two of you ever discuss aspects of your private sex lives?"

"Yes," Tara replied.

"Did you and Shayla ever mutually participate in any sexual acts together?"

"Yes we did," Tara replied as she stared directly at me.

"Can you please tell me the specifics of that mutual sex act that you and Ms. Coleman participated in?"

Tara smiled before she began talking. I just wanted to hop up outta my seat and charge that witness stand and slap the taste outta her mouth because I knew exactly where she was gonna go with her testimony.

"Well, first of all, there was more than one occasion where Shayla and I participated in sexual acts together. But there is one time in particular that really stands out in my mind."

Tara paused. She sat up in her chair and moved forward a bit. Anyone in the room could see my face turn to anger and disgust. I leaned over and I whispered in Andrea's ear and also into the assistant district attorney's ear.

"This is crazy because I know what she's gonna say and I was stone drunk that night."

Andrea patted me on my leg and told me not to worry. "We prepared for this, remember?"

Tara continued on: "Well, one night Shayla and myself and a few of our female friends had gone to a club to dance and party and have a good time. While we were at the club Shayla spotted a guy that was dancing and she told me that she was gonna get the guy to come back to my friend's apartment to have sex with her."

"Did Shayla know the guy?"

"No. He was just some guy, a random stranger."

"Well did this *random guy, this stranger,* if you will, that she picked up, did he in fact come back to your friend's apartment?"

"Yes he did."

"And what exactly happened at your friend's apartment?"

"Shayla proceeded to have sex with the guy in my friend's bedroom while me and another female friend of mines watched."

"How much time had passed from the time Shayla had met this gentleman in the club until she was at your house having sex with him?"

"No more than an hour and a half."

The defense attorney paused for dramatic effect. I was seething with anger. I just shook my head and I wanted to cry because I was feeling violated by the way he was painting me out to be.

"An hour and a half?" the lawyer screamed. His voice echoed throughout the courtroom.

"In an hour and a half Shayla Coleman meets some complete stranger in a night club, she takes him back to your friend's apartment, and she has sex with him?"

"Yes," Tara replied.

The lawyer paused again. "Did that *random guy* from the club wear any protection, any condoms?"

"No," Tara answered.

You fucking bitch! I wanted to yell at her. Even if I hadn't used any condoms that night, Tara knew damn good and well that I was way too drunk to even remember anything from that night, so how would I have known to tell the guy to put on a condom? She could have easily said that she wasn't sure if condoms had been used. Or she could have mentioned that I was drunk out of my mind. She was being malicious and purposely trying to train-wreck my chances of success in the trial.

"No condoms?" the lawyer shouted as he shook his head.

Then the lawyer went on to ask Tara about Pink Chocolate and about her working there as a stripper. Tara confirmed everything. He then asked her had I worked at Pink Chocolate and Tara told him yes, that I had worked there as a bartender.

"A bartender?" the lawyer said as he paused and then walked over to look at some papers that were on the defense table.

"Yes, I had to double-check Shayla Coleman's birthday. Shayla is not even twenty-one years old now, but yet, close to a year ago she was working at Pink Chocolate, an adult strip club as a bartender?"

"Well, when she got the job she used a fake driver's license in order to conceal her true age from the owners of Pink Chocolate," Tara so eloquently explained.

"I see," the lawyer said. "Probably the same fake driver's license that the police found on her possession on the night that Shayla Coleman alleges that she was raped."

Tara remained silent.

The lawyer then went in and asked Tara a bunch of questions about that night that I had been raped. He had her confirm that I had been

working at Pink Chocolate on that night, that I
hadn't been anywhere near Times Square like
I originally had said to the cops. He had her
confirm that I had lied and had her lie for me so
that no one would know where I had really been
coming from that night. He even had her tell how
I had paid her 15,000 dollars for going through
with the lie as planned.

"Did Shayla tell you anything about being
propositioned for sex by some of the male pa-
trons at Pink Chocolate on the night that she
alleges she was raped?"

"Yes. She told me that she had been paid three
hundred dollars by two men who had wanted her
to leave the club with them so that they could
have sex with her."

"Thank you, Tara." No further questions, Your
Honor.

I sat there and just stared at Tara and I shook
my head. I couldn't believe how she had played
me. But it was now her turn to be cross-examined by the assistant district attorney, a young,
feisty white chick named Jessica.

"Tara, on the night that Shayla supposedly
meets some random guy at the club and takes
him back to your friend's apartment to have sex
with him, had you been drinking that night?"

"We all had been—"

Jessica cut her off. "I asked you specifically, had *you* been drinking that night?"

"Yes."

"How much did you drink?"

"I don't remember," Tara said with an attitude.

"What were you drinking that night?"

"I don't know," Tara replied.

"So you remember drinking but you don't remember how much or what you were drinking? So how are you so clear on the sexual details that transpired between Shayla and this random guy?"

"Because things like that don't always happen, so you tend to remember those things more clearly."

Jessica nodded. "Well, do you remember Shayla drinking that night?"

"Yes."

"Had she drank more than you?"

"I don't know."

"So with the alcohol consumption, your memory is fuzzy but with the sexual details you remember specifics?"

Tara didn't say anything.

"Isn't it true, Tara, that you and your other female friend did more than just watch Tara have sex with this random guy?"

"No."

"No?" Jessica said with surprise in her voice. "You didn't engage in any lesbian sex acts that night?"

Tara looked a bit flustered and she twisted her lips and rolled her eyes, but she did say yes.

"So is it possible that while you were engaging in this lesbian sexual act that you may have been distracted and missed the fact that condoms had been used between Shayla and the guy?"

"I doubt it."

"Oh, you doubt it?" Jessica said. "I doubt it too. Because I believe that condoms were used."

Tara shrugged her shoulders.

"What does that shoulder shrug mean? Is that a stripper dance or something?"

"Your Honor, objection!" the defense lawyer yelled.

The judge then told Jessica to watch it.

"Now about the night that Shayla was raped. Well, actually before that. Didn't you help her to get the job as a bartender by putting in a good word for her?"

"Yes."

"And the two of you met when you were in high school. In fact, when you met, Shayla was only a freshman in high school and you yourself said that you were a few years older than her, so you had to know that she was too young to work as a bartender at that time."

"That's not true," Tara replied.

Jessica just looked at Tara as if to say *come on now*.

Then she added, "Did you leave Pink Chocolate with Shayla on the night that she was raped?"

"No."

"Do you know what time she left?"

"No."

"Did she in fact tell you that she had initially agreed to have sex for money but that she ultimately changed her mind before fully going through with it?"

"Maybe."

"Maybe? Either she did or she didn't!" Jessica yelled.

"Yes. Okay?"

"No further questions, Your Honor."

At that point Tara was told that she could step down from the witness stand since the defense did not want to ask her any additional questions.

Tara stepped off of the stand and as she walked to take her seat she mean-mugged me the entire time. I defiantly stared right back at her.

The judge spoke up and he gave everyone in the courtroom some verbal instructions. I wasn't paying close attention to what he was saying because it sounded like a bunch of legal mumbo jumbo that I wouldn't have understood anyway.

"You ready?" Andrea asked me. She broke me out of the trance that I had slipped into.

"I'm ready," I said, even though I had instantly become a ball of nerves.

Before I knew it, I had been called to take the witness stand. I approached the stand wearing all white. I had on white pants and a white top with open toe shoes that had a small white heel.

The courtroom was packed to standing room only and my heart pounded as I was giving my oath to tell the truth.

As soon as I sat down in my chair I looked at my aunt and she touched her heart and then she pointed toward heaven. I nodded at her and then I focused my attention on Jessica. Jessica was very calm and she spoke in a hushed tone that was designed to keep me calm.

Jessica asked me simple questions about myself, such as how old I was, what part of New York I was from, who I had grown up with, what I currently did for a living, what my future plans were as far as college and my career goals. I answered all of those questions with ease and I had gained my confidence being on the witness stand.

Then Jessica started to get more into the heart of things and she began asking me more personal and relevant, meaty questions. Specifically, she asked me about Pink Chocolate and how and why I had come to work there.

"I worked there basically to earn extra money. I knew it was only going to be a short-term thing because I was waiting on a large sum of money from my mother's insurance policy and I just needed some money in the meantime to hold me over until my settlement check came."

"I understand," Jessica said.

"Did you ever have any aspirations of being a nude dancer or a stripper?"

"None at all."

"Explain why you simply didn't go to a Burger King or a McDonald's for a job instead of seeking to work as a bartender at a strip club."

"Well, at the time Tara was my best friend and I guess it was her influence that sort of nudged me in that direction. Had I had friends who were working at a Burger King or at McDonald's then I guess those would have been my influences and I probably would have chosen to work at those types of establishments. Looking back, I can definitely say that I wish I had chosen the fast-food route."

Jessica smiled at my comments. Then she asked me to recount exactly what had happened in terms of me being propositioned by the defendant Antonio Reid.

I went on to explain that it was Antonio Reid's friend who had propositioned me and that Antonio Reid had simply played the background in another part of the strip club. I told how his friend had paid me three hundred dollars and disguised it as if he were paying for expensive bottles of liquor. Then I told the courtroom how I had gotten really nervous and had second thoughts about going through with the whole thing and so I rushed out of the strip club as quickly as I could with plans of never coming back. I stopped speaking after I told the court how unfortunately my plans didn't work out, because the defendant and his friend had gotten wind of my plan to ditch them and before I could get into my car they accosted me.

"And after they accosted you, can you tell the jury what happened after that point?"

I paused, not for dramatic effect or anything like that, but I just wanted to gather my thoughts and to make sure that I was ready to speak clearly and articulately so that everyone could finally publicly hear my side of what had happened.

I went on to tell the jury step-by-step what had happened to me and how I was raped in the backseat of the Suburban truck. As I spoke tears came to my eyes. I could also see my aunt wiping away tears from her eyes.

"And so you were dumped out of the Suburban and just left for dead until the police were notified and you were taken into the hospital."

"Yes, that's correct."

"Shayla, please explain to the jury why you initially told the police that you were coming from Times Square, when in actuality you had really been coming from Pink Chocolate?"

I turned my lips and sighed as I shook my head. I looked dead-on at the jury and I started to explain my reasons behind what I had done.

At that point I began to cry as I explained to the jury that deep down inside I was trying to avoid disappointing my dad. I knew had my dad—or anyone else, for that matter—known that I had really been working at a strip club and that was where I was coming from that night, I knew that no one would believe my story about me being raped.

"So tell the jury now, do you see the man who raped you that night?"

"Yes," I confidently said.

"Can you point to him?"

I extended my right arm and my index finger and I pointed to Antonio Reid, who was seated at the defense table in a dark blue double-breasted suit. He shook his head as I pointed at him.

"You picked Antonio Reid out of a mug-shot book and out of a lineup, is that correct?"

"Yes."

"Are you as sure now as you were when you picked him out of that mug-shot book and that lineup that he is the man who raped you?"

"Yes. I am one hundred percent sure!" I said with all kinds of confidence.

"Thank you. No further questions, Your Honor."

I blew out a lot of air and I exhaled. I felt very good at that point about how I was coming across to the jurors. I looked at my aunt and she gave me the thumbs-up sign.

The defense attorney then began to cross-examine me, and immediately I knew that his entire tone and demeanor was gonna be different than that of Jessica's. He wasted no time and he came out swinging.

"Shayla, how old were you when you lost your virginity?"

"Objection! Your Honor, that is irrelevant," Jessica stood up and shouted.

"Objection overruled. Ms. Coleman, please answer the question."

I paused and my heart was pounding. I looked over at Andrea and she nodded her head up and down at me.

"Well, when I was nine years old I—"

The entire courtroom gasped. I didn't even get a chance to finish my statement and explain the situation with my nanny.

The judged banged his gavel and told everyone in the courtroom to please cooperate and to not make any noises.

"Can you say that a little louder so that the jury can hear you?"

"When I was nine years old I—" I spoke up and said. I could tell I was slipping into fight mode and I wanted to punch that lawyer in his mouth because he purposely cut me off and interrupted me and wouldn't let me finish my statement.

"Nine years old. Okay. So how many sexual partners have you had since that time?"

"I don't know," I said with an attitude.

"You don't know because you lost count?" the lawyer asked me.

"No, I don't know because there was no need to keep a count."

"The last witness gave testimony that you had sex with a random guy that you met at a club and who you didn't even know for two hours. Now is that a practice that you engage in regularly?"

"No."

"No? Well, why on that particular night?"

"Actually, I don't even remember having sex with a random guy that night."

"Oh, you don't remember. Is that similar to how you don't remember how many sexual partners you've had? Ms. Coleman, come on. You're not even nineteen years old and you can't remember how many sexual partners you've had?"

I didn't say anything but a tear began to roll down my cheek.

"Tell me about your father."

"What about him?" I said through my tears.

"Well, for starters, is he here today in this courtroom?"

"No."

"Why not?"

"Ask him! I don't know!"

"A few minutes ago you said you had knowingly lied to police so that you wouldn't have to tell the truth and disappoint your father. It would seem to me that you are close to your father and that he would be here. So, are you close to your father?"

"No."

"No?" the lawyer asked with a huge question mark.

"No," I said a second time.

The lawyer shook his head. "So you were worried about disappointing your dad and you're not even close to your dad? Shayla, there is a man sitting right there—Antonio Reid—he has a life and a bright future ahead of him, he's engaged, he has two children, he has a good job, and your web of lies are turning this man's life upside down!"

"Objection—Your Honor, this is ridiculous," Jessica vented.

The judge told the lawyer to watch his statements and to keep his line of questions specific.

"Do you want to have a good relationship with your father?"

"Yes, I would like to."

"Did you think that by saying that you were raped that would bring your father closer to you and make your relationship with him better?"

"No."

The lawyer paused and he stared at me.

"You lied to get the job at Pink Chocolate, is that correct?"

"Yes."

"You lied to the police and said that you had been assaulted and raped after leaving a Times Square movie theater, is that correct?"

"Yes."

"You asked your friend Tara to lie to the police for you to make the story that you had given them sound believable. Is that correct?"

"Yes."

"You just stated a minute ago that you didn't remember that night of having random sex with a guy you had known for less than two hours, is that correct?"

"Yes, but because I had been drinking."

"Oh, you had been drinking. So did that cause a lapse in memory?"

"Possibly."

"Well, had you been drinking on the night that you claim you were raped?"

"Yes, but—"

"Yes, indeed. You were drinking that night!" the lawyer screamed and cut me off in the middle of my words.

"Let's get this straight: At eighteen years old you can't remember how many sexual partners you've had, you've admitted that you started having sex at the age of nine years old, you have admitted to repeated lies. You admitted that you've had a lapse in memory when you were drinking and now you want this jury to believe that this innocent man raped you?"

I kept quiet and didn't say anything.

"Shayla, are you a promiscuous woman?"

"No!"

"Did you have a promiscuous past?" the lawyer asked as he got right up in my face.

"Yes, but it wasn't my fault!" I screamed as tears started rolling down my eyes.

"So you're not a promiscuous woman but you've had a promiscuous past? No further questions, Your Honor," the defense lawyer said.

Jessica immediately got up, walked over to me and handed me a tissue.

After I regained my composure she began to ask questions so that she could clean up the damage that the defense attorney had done to my credibility. Thankfully, Jessica cleaned things up in a quick, clean, and painless way and I was soon off of the witness stand and back at the prosecutor's table.

Antonio Reid was called to the stand next. His lawyer basically tried to defend him by sticking to the alibi that Antonio Reid had originally given and also by focusing on how he had moved away from his criminal past and was a devoted father and soon-to-be-husband.

When Jessica cross-examined him she poked all kinds of holes into his story. She asked him had he

ever been to the Pink Chocolate strip club, which
he admitted that he had. She asked him had he
ever been physically abusive toward a woman before in the past and he admitted that he had.

Overall he did an excellent job to help save
his ass. He never got flustered at any point during his stint on the witness stand and that could
have been because he had a packed courtroom
full of supporters to draw strength from.

The third day and the final day of the trial con-
sisted of expert testimony of people in the medi-
cal field and the forensic specialist. They were
brought in by the prosecution to help illustrate
for the jury how rare Antonio Reid's blood type
was and the differences in blood types in general
and why they felt strongly, based on statistics
and odds, that Antonio Reid was indeed the person who raped me.

After the experts witnesses were finished, it
was time for closing arguments and I have to admit that both sides gave great closing arguments.
The defense begged the jury to see through me
and see that I was not credible based on the
admitted lies that had come out of my mouth.
They also begged the jury to see through the
prosecution's probability theories. The defense

told the jury that unless there was a one hundred percent probability, then everything else could be thrown out the window because anything less than one hundred percent equated to reasonable doubt.

When Jessica spoke during her closing arguments, she reminded me of an A-list actress with her passion. She pointed out to the jury that yes, I had lied, but I'd admitted that before I was caught lying, which showed my true nature to voluntarily have the truth exposed. She said had I been caught lying instead of being straightforward after having told my fibs then no one would really know if I was being genuinely contrite or if I was being contrite simply because I was caught not telling the truth.

Jessica also asked the jury to use common sense when they looked at the probabilities. First, she told them to remember that the movie that Antonio Reid had gone to see—which no one was doubting—was a movie that had ended in more than enough time for him to make it to Pink Chocolate before I had left. She asked the jury not to forget that Antonio Reid had been to the strip club in the past and that he had been violent toward women in the past.

But the most powerful part of Jessica's closing arguments was when she dug into her pocket and she pulled out a dollar bill and a lottery ticket. She proceeded to tell the jury that if each of them were to wager one dollar on the lottery that the likelihood of any of them winning the lottery was slim to none.

"Why would your chances be so slim?" Jessica calmly asked the jury. "Based on the *probabilities,* that's why!" She then paused and gathered her words and thoughts.

"The defense wants you to ignore the rare probabilities that exist in this rape case. But I tell you that you cannot ignore probabilities. And if any of you think that you can go out *today* and play the lottery and win, then don't convict Antonio Reid in this rape case. But if you don't think that you can go out today and win the lottery, then I say that you have an obligation and a duty to convict Antonio Reid simply because you understand long odds and probabilities. With both the probabilities and with the evidence that has been presented to you over the course of the past three days, I urge you and plead with you to do the right thing and convict Antonio Reid for the vicious criminal act that was perpetrated on this beautiful young lady that you see sitting right there at that table."

With that both sides rested. The case went to the jury.

All anyone could do at that point was wait for the jury to deliberate and to come back with a verdict.

Chapter Twenty-four

Kwame

Two days had passed and the jury was still deliberating. They had deliberated all day Thursday and all day Friday and they still hadn't reached a verdict. The rule of thumb was that when juries reached quick verdicts it usually meant a conviction. On the flip side, when juries deliberate for too long it usually meant that they would come back with an acquittal.

I was a nervous wreck the entire time during deliberations. With the weekend coming up it meant that the jury wouldn't be resuming deliberations until that upcoming Monday. Andrea assured me that I didn't have anything to worry about. She told me to go home and try my best to relax.

My aunt wanted me to come by her house for the weekend but I declined. I would have loved to have chilled with my aunt, but the truth was that I had never really mended things with my cousin Earl and it would have just been awkward as hell being around him.

So I went home and tried my best to relax. After taking a shower and cooking something to eat I chilled on my sofa and started watching music videos. And at about ten o'clock that night, just as I was dozing off, my phone rang.

"Hello," I said into the cordless handset.

"Hello, can I speak to Shayla?" a male voice asked.

I was feeling really sleepy and I didn't recognize the voice. I sat up a bit and tried to be more alert.

"Speaking."

"Hey Shayla, I don't know if you remember me, but this is Kwame. I met you when you came down to Howard for a tour a couple of weeks ago?"

There was a pause of silence as I tried my best to remember who this Kwame was.

"You don't remember me? I was the one who introduced myself to you just before you were about to get in your car."

"Oh, okay," I said as a smile plastered across my face.

There was some more silence.

"So, you do remember who I am?"

"Yeah, of course I remember you. What threw me off was that I just didn't remember giving anybody my number when I was down there," I replied.

"Well, actually you didn't give me your number. I've done some detective work every day since I'd met you, trying to get ahold of your number."

I chuckled into the phone.

"Detective work? Well, why didn't you just ask me for my number when you introduced yourself to me that day?"

"I wanted to but honestly you intimidated a nigga."

"Me?" I laughed and said, "I was nice to everybody that weekend."

"Yeah I know, but I mean, you look all attractive and sexy, your gear was all top-of-the-line designers and you was getting into a Mercedes-Benz. I'm just some down-south country nigga and I thought you would just brush me off."

I felt flattered at that moment and a big smile came across my face. I chuckled again. "Nah, I am so not like that."

There was more silence on the phone and I could sense that Kwame was somewhat shy and didn't have much game, so I spoke up.

"Okay, so now you got me on the phone, so what's up?"

"Well, I know that classes start in two weeks and I just wanted to put my bid in early and see if I can get first dibs on taking you out to eat or to the movies or something like that."

A girlie, tingly feeling came over me when Kwame asked me that. It was the first time in my life that a guy had straight-up asked to take me out. I mean, guys had asked to get with me and they were usually straight-up and blunt about their intentions, but never had anyone asked me out in the traditional sense.

"If you went through all kinds of trouble to get my number, well then, of course you can take me out. I feel special."

I could tell that Kwame was smiling on the other end of the phone as he began to speak.

"Yo, you don't know how hard that was for me to ask you that. I mean, the worst thing that you could have said was no. But I just think that you are so beautiful and I would've been crushed if you had said no."

"Aww, that's so sweet," I replied.

"So you're from New York, right?"

"Yeah, and you?"

"Oh, I'm from South Carolina but I like D.C. much better and I stayed here this summer after my freshman year was complete."

"Oh, okay," I replied.

"So can I give you my number?" Kwame asked.

He proceeded to give me his number and I gave him my cell phone number. I also told him that he could call me back before school started if he wanted too. We ended our conversation and I got off the phone feeling all warm and fuzzy and excited.

I got up and I went to my kitchen. Although I had told myself that I would stop drinking, I convinced myself that it was okay for me to have one drink in order to unwind from the trial. So I poured myself my favorite drink, which was Bacardi and Coke.

Yeah, a few days prior, I had lost my will to resist alcohol and I broke my vow of not keeping alcohol in my house. I had gone and purchased a gallon-sized bottle of Bacardi.

I drank that one drink that I had poured for myself and before I knew it that one drink had turned into three drinks and those three drinks had turned into six drinks and I found myself buzzing and happy as hell. Only now that I was buzzing I had to find an outlet for that nice feeling that I was experiencing.

What I ended up doing was I returned to what was familiar to me and what had been my outlet for so long, and that was sex. I grabbed my cable remote control and I searched for the adult pay-per-view channels. Immediately I got on the phone with the cable company and I ordered an adult movie.

Less than five minutes into the movie I found myself masturbating on my living room sofa. As the movie played I continued to drink my Bacardi and Coke, which gave me the courage to keep watching the movie. After I'd watched one movie I ordered another movie and then another one after that.

By the time it was two o'clock in the morning I was good and drunk. Since I had masturbated and had had a total of six orgasms, my body was feeling all tingly and good and I felt as if I didn't have a care in the world.

As I prepared to fall asleep right there on the sofa with a porno movie playing in the background, I decided that I really didn't care what the verdict in my rape case would be. As long as I had sex and liquor I knew that I would always be all right. I also wondered about Kwame and if he was packing or not and would he be any good in bed. In fact, I couldn't wait to get to school to see him so that I could give him some and find out firsthand exactly what he was working with.

Chapter Twenty-five

The Verdict

That following Monday my phone began ringing at 5:00 A.M. It was Andrea. She had called to wake me up to ensure that I would be at her office by 8:00 that morning.

"You up?" Andrea asked me.

"Not really," I replied. I was groggy as all hell. My Friday night drinking had turned into a weekend of binge drinking and masturbating. So at 5:00 A.M. that Monday morning I was still feeling hungover.

"Well, get up. The verdict should be in sometime this morning."

I didn't reply to her. My head was pounding.

"Shayla? Get up, girl!"

"Andrea, I don't feel good," I groaned through the phone.

"What's wrong?"

I kept quiet.

Andrea didn't immediately respond so I spoke up.

"I feel hungover."

Andrea again didn't immediately respond.

I sucked my teeth and said, "I'm just tired of all this court bullshit! I'm tired of my father's tired ass! I'm tired of phony mothafuckas! I'm tired of trying to be something that I'm not destined to be."

"What are you destined to be?" Andrea asked.

"Andrea, you know what, no disrespect, but I don't know and I really don't care."

"Shayla, look, baby, it's probably just your nerves, you know, thinking about the verdict and all. Get up. Get dressed and I'll send a car to come get you."

I blew some air into the phone.

"Come on, Shayla, it's the last day. I promise you the verdict is gonna come in today and it'll be all over."

I chuckled as I tried to sit up in my bed. "You know what? Can I just be honest with you about how I feel?"

Andrea didn't say anything.

"I don't care about the fucking verdict! I don't care about college! I don't care about none of that shit!"

"So what do you care about? No, matter of fact, let me tell you what you care about, Shayla. All you care about is laying up with somebody so you can trick yourself into thinking that that person loves you and thinking that they give a shit about you. And if I'm lying, then you stop me. But what you wanna do is go out and get some dick and bury your issues in sex and then get drunk and high so you won't have to think about the sex you shouldn't have had. And when you recover from your hangover and the medicated feelings of being high, you'll wanna get some more dick to start the cycle all over again. Shayla, I can shoot straight with you because I've been there and I've done that. Now I'm telling you what you gotta do is get up outta that bed. Get dressed and when the car comes for you I want you to come down here and look into the eyes of the man who raped you while the jury tells him he's guilty."

I sat up in the bed and my eyes were as wide as the moon. I definitely hadn't expected Andrea to respond to me like that.

"But what if they find him innocent?"

"Then if they do you and I will pick up the pieces and we'll get through this together. But that's not gonna happen, Shayla. And what else is not gonna happen is you're not gonna lay around thinking the worst of yourself. And you're damn sure not gonna be laying around trying to fuck your problems away."

I was quiet and I was shocked at the way Andrea was talking. I didn't know what to say so I kept my mouth shut.

"If you're hungover, it's all right. Just do the best you can to get yourself together and I'll have the car there for you in one hour. Okay?"

I blew some more air into the phone before saying okay.

"And Shayla, I wanna tell you something else."

"What?"

"I love you. And we're gonna get through this thing today and then you're gonna go off to college and make things happen for yourself. All right?"

"Yeah."

I got off the phone with Andrea and I peeled myself out of bed. Somehow I willed myself into the shower and I got myself ready within an hour. A Lincoln Continental was waiting for me downstairs in front of my building and I hopped in and was whisked away to Andrea's office. By the time I reached her office it was only seven o'clock in the morning and most people hadn't come in to work yet, which was good because I still felt like shit.

"You don't look too bad. Matter of fact, you look good," Andrea said to me as I came into her office.

"Yeah, but I don't feel good," I said with a mini-smile plastered across my face.

"Close the door."

I closed the door and I sat down.

"So what happened to you?"

I shook my head and I proceeded to tell her how I had went on a drinking binge throughout the weekend.

"The weekend is gone and we're not gonna get that time back so it doesn't make sense to harp over what we can't change. But I can tell you this. Binges like that are gonna keep happening and the consequences that go along with it are gonna be more and more serious. What you gotta do in times like this weekend is pick up the phone and call me. I'm here for you but you gotta reach out to me if you wanna stay on the right track."

I nodded and I smiled because I was expecting Andrea to come down on me and abuse me verbally, but she didn't.

"Now, Shayla, it was hard for me to hold this in since Friday, but the jury reached a verdict late Friday at around six-thirty."

My heart started beating and I sat up in my chair.

"Before you ask me, I don't know what the verdict is. I just know that it's been reached. But since it was so late on Friday we decided to just hold everything off until Monday morning."

"Wow," I said as I stood up and walked around the room.

"Don't be nervous."

"I'm not nervous. It's just that it seems like everything is hinging on this verdict."

"Everything like what?"

"Like being vindicated. Especially being vindicated in my father's eyes and being vindicated in everybody else's eyes, for that matter."

Andrea nodded.

"I mean, I know what happened to me that night. And I know Antonio Reid is the guy who raped me but if the jury doesn't believe my story then I'm just gonna continue to be looked at as this fast-ass promiscuous chick who was just looking for it and got more than she could handle."

Andrea and I continued to talk and we also ate the continental breakfast that she had in her office. Between still feeling hungover and with my nerves on edge I barely ate or drank anything. Fortunately for me, time flew by and by nine-thirty that morning, I found myself in a packed courtroom.

The media was there in full force. Antonio Reid seemed as if he had paid his friends and family to come down and support him. The courtroom was packed with his supporters. I couldn't help but feel like all of the eyes in the entire courtroom were on me. But thankfully, I did have a few supporters, namely my Aunt Tanisha and her husband and all of their kids, all of them except for Earl. But what shocked me the most wasn't that my father hadn't shown up, it was the fact that his girlfriend had. Yup, she was sitting right in the front row in front with my aunt.

I sat with a blank look on my face and I looked straight ahead. The judge soon entered the courtroom and my heart began to beat even faster. Andrea rubbed me on my leg and she grabbed hold of my sweaty, clammy hands.

At that point the only thing that I could think about was my mom. I wondered if she was able to see what was going on.

Then the jury was brought into the courtroom.

The judge brought order to the court and then he began giving instructions to the courtroom and to the jury. When he was done with his instructions I knew that the moment of truth was finally there. He asked the jury had they reached a verdict. After they told him that they had, the judge then asked the defendant to stand.

Andrea tapped me on my leg and she nodded for me to look toward Antonio Reid.

I looked at him and he also looked at me. He stood clasping his hands, which were behind his back. He didn't look at me for too long as he turned his attention to the judge and then to the jury forewoman.

"For the charge of rape in the first degree, do you find the defendant Antonio Reid guilty or not guilty?"

My heart couldn't beat any faster and my mouth was dry as a desert.

"We find the defendant guilty," the petite forewoman said in a calm and quiet voice.

"I told you, baby! We did it!" Andrea whispered into my ear as she and the whole prosecution team embraced me in a group hug.

"Yo, this is some bullshit! That ho is lying!" somebody screamed from the audience.

I also heard loud crying coming from a woman in the front row. After the embrace was over I looked and saw that it was Antonio Reid's fiancée who was crying. Drowning out her tears and what took my attention away from her was the loud jeering that continued to come from all of Antonio Reid's supporters who were in the courtroom.

The thing that I remembered hearing the most throughout the loud throng of voices were the words *bitch*, *whore*, *slut*, and *tramp*. I have to admit that the reaction from everybody really made me feel like shit. It also made me wonder had I done the right thing by going through with the whole trial.

The judge tried his best to restore order to the court but things had turned into an absolute zoo and there was complete pandemonium.

Antonio Reid had sat back down and he had his face buried in both of his hands. I couldn't see his eyes but I could tell that he was clearly sobbing.

Wow, I thought to myself. I had never in my life seen a grown-ass man sobbing like that.

Andrea rubbed my back and I blew out air from my lungs. My heart had finally stopped beating so fast as the reality began to sink in that the trial was in fact finally over.

The judge was finally able to restore order to the court and he said some further things to the jury before he addressed the defense. Since Antonio Reid had not been able to make bail the judge ordered that he immediately begin serving his sentence. He instructed the court officers to handcuff him and escort him out of the courtroom.

More jeers began to come from the crowd and the judge banged his gavel and instructed everyone on when the official sentencing would be.

The court officers asked Antonio to stand so that they could place handcuffs on him. At that point I was able to see the redness in his eyes and the moistness on his face from the tears.

"It's gonna be all right, Antonio," someone shouted.

"We love you, boo. Keep ya head up," someone else shouted.

Antonio had his hands cuffed behind his back and before he was led out of the courtroom he turned and looked at me but he didn't say anything. Then he looked at his fiancée and he mouthed the words that he loved her.

"I love you too baby," she said.

Just as Antonio was about to walk past the judge he said to him, "Your Honor, she knows in her heart that I didn't rape her."

Then he turned and looked at me as the court officers yanked his arms as if he was a dog and they were pulling on his leash.

"You know it wasn't me," he said to me.

I looked at him and a smirk mixed with a smile came across my face. I knew that all Antonio Reid was trying to do was play mind games with me. He had raped me, he'd been caught, tried, and convicted, yet he was still trying to come out on top by playing with my head.

"Nigga, it was you!" I shot back and said with a whole bunch of attitude. I made sure that he heard me just before he disappeared out of eyesight behind a thick security door.

Andrea and the prosecutor told me to hush and not say anything.

"He don't have any power over you. Don't waist your energy. The jury found him guilty and that's all that matters," Andrea whispered into my ear.

Yeah, that is all that matters, I told myself.

Finally, I felt like I had been vindicated. I was desperately hoping that that sense of vindication would begin to change things around for me in my life. Unfortunately, though, that feeling of vindication wouldn't last forever.

Chapter Twenty-six

School Daze

Two weeks after the trial ended I headed off to start Howard University. I had mixed emotions about leaving New York. On one hand, I was eager to leave because I looked at starting college as a chance to have a fresh new start on everything. On the other hand, I was scared to leave what had been familiar to me.

I gave up my apartment in New York because I would be renting an apartment down in D.C. I hated to give up my apartment but it was time to move on to new things. Fortunately for me, I still had that twenty-something thousand dollars from the insurance money that I hadn't squandered and I also had managed to save another 5,000 dollars from the job that I had. My boss had also told me that he would be able to hook me up with a job in D.C. if I wanted to work during the summer and during the winter and spring breaks. So as far as money, I knew that I would be good.

Andrea and I had hung out the day before I left for school and she gave me one of her usual inspiring talks. She also insisted that I call her on a regular basis to let her know how I was making out.

I promised her that I would.

The thing that really tore me apart about leaving for school was the fact that my father had finally given in and called me to wish me well. I felt torn because I didn't know if by him calling me it meant that he was trying to mend things and include me in his life again. If so, how would that work out now that I would be off and leaving for school, hundreds of miles from New York.

The day that my phone rang and my father's number appeared on the caller ID, I immediately thought that it was his girlfriend calling. To my surprise and complete shock it was my father on the other end of the line.

"Hey Shayla, this is Daddy."

I paused when I heard his voice because I didn't know what to say.

My father broke the silence and he asked me how was I doing.

"I'm doing okay," I answered. I didn't know whether to smile or to be angry.

"Your aunt told me that you would be leaving for school tomorrow and I wanted to make sure that you were okay. Do you need help moving your stuff or anything?"

"No, I hired this moving and storage company and they are taking care of all of that for me."

There was some more awkward silence.

"I had been trying to call you. Where you been?"

"I've been around. You know, just handling and taking care of business."

"I was hoping that you would have come to court during the trial but—"

My father cut me off. "Baby, I know you wanted me there. But you know what? You're gonna be nineteen in a few weeks. You're not my little girl anymore. You're a grown woman and you gotta fend for yourself."

I slowly nodded my head on the other end of the phone and I twisted up my lips because I knew that this conversation wouldn't flow the way that I had wished it would have flowed.

"Yeah, I know, it's just that when they read the verdict I would have given anything for you to have been by my side."

My father didn't say anything. I knew that part of the reason he didn't say anything was because of his pride and his stubbornness in knowing that the jury had vindicated me and all the while in his heart he thought that I had fabricated the whole rape thing.

"So you ready for college?" he asked, blatantly changing the subject.

"I think so."

My heart started to pound because I knew that the conversation wouldn't last for much longer. There was just one thing that I needed to hear my father say, but I was nervous about asking him.

"You'll do fine. You're grown now and you know how to handle yourself," my father said. He was so superficial.

My palms got really sweaty and I inhaled a bunch of air. I held it in my lungs for what seemed to be five minutes before slowly letting it seep out.

"Daddy, are you proud of me?"

My heart began to pound with anxious anticipation of my father's answer.

"Am I proud of you?"

"Yes. Are you?"

I could hear my father begin to chuckle on the other end of the phone.

"Shayla, come on now."

"Come on what?"

"I'm calling to wish you well and see if you need anything. And it's like every time we talk it's always some shit."

My face frowned up and I instantly got angry, but I caught myself because after all, my father had reached out to me. I didn't know his true intentions or if he was being genuine. I did want to keep the future lines of communication open, so I knew that right then and there it was time to just end the conversation.

"Daddy, thanks for calling me. My friend is ringing my intercom right now; she's downstairs in the lobby and I don't want her to be waiting on me. We're gonna run to the mall to get some last-minute stuff. But thanks for calling me and I'll call you when I get settled in to let you know how I'm making out."

"Oh, okay. Yeah, no problem."

"All right, so I'll speak to you later," I said. I really didn't want to get off the phone but I knew that it would be best that I did.

"Daddy, I love you," I said, shocking myself.

"I know you do, Shayla. And just remember what I told you earlier. You're not Daddy's little girl anymore. So you gotta be tough and learn to fend for yourself."

I blew some air into the phone. "Okay, I won't forget."

I paused before telling my father that I had to go.

My father said good-bye and the conversation ended there. I wanted to scream out in frustration but I kept my composure. Right then and there I convinced myself that my father did in fact love me and he was proud of me, otherwise he wouldn't have called me.

At least that's what I wanted to believe.

During my first week at Howard University I knew that I was gonna like being a college student. I took to the whole spirit of the college and I made a lot of friends, both male and female, during my first week. Definitely the thing that I liked most was the parties that I'd gone to that first Friday and Saturday night.

I became cool with this girl named Kenya from my business law class. Kenya was a sophomore from Detroit and she was also a Delta. She had invited me to a party that the Deltas were having that Friday night. I jumped at the chance to go, but the mistake that I made was I'd told Kwame where I was going. I added to my mistake by telling him that it was okay for him to go with me to the party.

Kwame was cool and he was a cutie but what I didn't know was that he didn't know how to come to a party with a chick and still mingle so that I could do me and he could do him. Nah, none of that, Kwame was smothering my ass the entire night at the party, the nigga wouldn't let me breathe.

There were all kinds of cuties walking around who I wanted to meet but that was not gonna happen with Kwame practically hanging onto me.

"Kenya, you gotta help me ditch this bug-a-boo," I whispered loudly over the music into her ear.

Kenya turned and looked at Kwame.

"Hello, I'm Kenya," she said as she extended her hand to him.

Kwame shook her hand, smiled, and told her that it was nice to meet her.

"Kwame, I'll be right back. I'm going to the bathroom," I said as I grabbed Kenya by the hand and led her in the direction of the bathroom.

"Girl, he's cute! Why you trying to ditch him?"

"'Cause I didn't know the nigga was gonna be up under me the whole night. There's way too many other cuties up in here for him to be playing me so close like he's my fucking man or something."

Kenya laughed.

"Look, just tell him straight-up to let you breathe a little."

I thought for a minute and then I came up with my plan. I knew that all I needed was some liquor in me to loosen me up so I could do me without caring about Kwame. I told Kenya that I was gonna have Kwame run with me to the liquor store and hopefully I would be able to ditch him then.

"Girl we gotchu! You ain't gotta run to no liquor store," said, laughing at me.

"They serving drinks in here?"

"No, but me and my soros got our own stash. Just go in the bathroom and chill for a minute. I'll meet you in there."

I excitedly made my way to the bathroom in my tight jeans and high heels and just as I was about the push the bathroom door open I heard Kwame calling my name.

"Shayla!"

Oh Dayu, I screamed in my head. I turned around and fully faced Kwame but I didn't say anything because I knew if I had, I would have simply screamed at him and I didn't wanna hurt his feelings or embarrass him.

"You okay?" he asked.

I smiled and slowly shook my head. "Uh, yeah," I said as I raised my eyebrows.

"Oh, okay, so I'll wait here for you to come out."

"No. Kwame, look, I'm a big girl. You ain't gotta wait for me like I'm in first grade going to use the potty or something."

Kwame laughed. "Nah, it's okay. I don't mind."

Ugh! I was about to lose it. I didn't say anything and I just turned and made my way into the bathroom.

Two minutes later Kenya walked into the bathroom and she immediately burst out laughing as soon as she saw me.

"You see what the hell I mean now?" I shouted at her. "Yo that nigga is gonna drive me fucking crazy."

"Oh my God, Shayla, that ain't normal, the nigga got stalker tendencies." Kenya laughed and said, "Here, I know you need this."

Kenya handed me a sixteen-ounce container of cranberry juice that she said was mixed with vodka. I took the drink from her hand and I guzzled it down like I was dehydrated and on a desert.

"Girl, you gonna be throwing up. You can't drink that fast," Kenya warned me.

I smiled and I shook my head to tell her that I would be all right.

"You smoke?" I asked her.

"Weed?"

"Yeah."

"Nah I don't but my some of my girls do. Why, you want some weed?"

"Well, first let me go back out here and see how this nigga is acting and then I'll let you know."

Kenya and I made our way out of the bathroom to head back to the party. There Kwame was standing front and center waiting for me. Kenya burst out laughing and she told me that she would see me later. Thankfully, the first effects of the vodka and cranberry juice was kicking in.

"Come on. Dance with me," I said to Kwame as I grabbed him by the hand and led him to the dance floor.

I took Kwame to the middle of the dance floor and I began grinding on him as the DJ played reggae music. He had rhythm but I could tell that he wasn't that comfortable and he wasn't letting himself go on the dance floor.

"What's the matter? You scared of me or something?" I asked him.

Kwame shook his head no and he continued to dance with me.

We danced through two more reggae songs. While I was dancing Kenya came up to me and tapped me on the shoulder.

"Okay, girl, time to cut the zero and get with a hero."

I smiled and looked at her to ask her what she was talking about.

"One of the Q's was asking me about you and he wants to meet you."

"Is he cute?" I whispered in Kenya's ear, smiling.

Based on Kenya's look I could tell that I had asked a stupid question so I told her to give me about a half an hour to forty-five minutes so that I could permanently ditch Kwame.

As soon as Kenya walked away I turned toward Kwame and I pulled him close to me. "So you're not scared of me?"

"No."

I pulled him even closer to me and I began to tongue kiss him right there on the floor.

To my surprise the kiss was off the hook. Kwame definitely knew how to move his tongue and his body felt really good pressed up against mine. When we finished kissing I looked at Kwame and smiled and then the two of us continued to dance. The DJ switched up the music and threw on hip-hop records.

After dancing through three hip-hop songs I grabbed him by the hand and began to lead him out of the party.

"Where you taking me to?" he asked.

"Just come on."

I didn't tell Kwame at that moment, but my plan was to take him back to my apartment and sex him. Although he was a bug-a-boo, he had piqued my interest ever since he had called me prior to school starting. To me there was no sense in beating around the bush and dragging things out. I knew what he was really after and I was curious as hell to see what he was working with. Plus, I figured the best way to ditch him without him getting offended would be if I took him back to my room and fucked him and then dropped him back off at his place when we were done. That way I could make it back to the party and everything would be all good.

So we made it to my Benz and got in. Kwame was still questioning me as to where I was taking him.

Nigga, is you that slow? I wanted to ask him.

"We going back to my apartment," I said while turning on the radio.

Kwame didn't say anything as he sat in the passenger seat in his tan Timbs and dark blue jeans. He also had on this nice-fitting black shirt that showed off his muscles. I couldn't wait to see him with his shirt off.

That vodka still had my head feeling nice and I rocked my body to the rhythm of the music. Kwame was still not saying anything and I wondered if he was still feeling intimidated by me.

"Kwame, I'm sorry, I should have asked you if you wanted to drive."

"Your car?" he asked.

"Yeah, you want me to pull over so that you can drive?"

Kwame shook his head no and he continued to sit in silence. We were only about twenty blocks or so away from my apartment and I wanted to hurry up and get there. I didn't feel like messing up the buzz that I had by playing psychologist to Kwame, but I could sense that something was eating him.

Maybe he heard what Kenya said to me, I thought

"You all right?" I asked him as I turned down the music.

"Yeah, I'm okay. But can I ask you something?"

I nodded my head and I just knew that he was gonna ask me about what Kenya had said about the cute Q-dog.

"Were you drinking?"

"Yeah. Why? You wanna stop by the liquor store?"

Kwame chuckled and shook his head. Then he began to sort of lecture me about drinking and how I need to be careful.

Oh, here we go, I thought.

"So you don't drink?" I asked.

We were just pulling into my apartment complex and I was attempting to maneuver my car into my parking space.

"Oh, that's cool. I can respect that," I said.

I put the car in park and let it sit idle. I paused before turning the car off. I could just feel my buzz totally leaving me.

I turned the engine off, I took the key out of the ignition and opened my door. Kwame didn't move and he stayed in his seat.

"Come on," I said to him.

I couldn't believe how the nigga had been all up under me at the party and now at the moment of truth he was dillydallying around and taking his time.

"Shayla, I can't go inside with you."

"What are you talking about? Just come on."

"Nah, what I'm saying is, you was drinking, we already kissed, and I know if we go inside your apartment right now that something is gonna go down."

I wanted to sarcastically say, *you think?*

But I smiled and I shook my head. I was trying to figure out if this was part of Kwame's game. I didn't know how to respond because I had never been in a situation before where a guy was making it seem as if he was trying to *not* get in my pants.

"Kwame, just come on. I'm sorry if I intimidate you or something, but trust me, everything is all good."

"Nah, Shayla, everything ain't all good. I mean, I really like you, you attractive and all that, but the thing is, I can't get with you like that."

My pussy had stopped throbbing and now Kwame had managed to not only ruin my buzz but he also was ruining my sexual appetite.

"Wow. You really playing me right now," I said to him as I sat back in the driver's seat.

"I never told you this, but my father is a pastor and I'm really into the church and going upstairs with you to your apartment and having sex with you would just go against everything I believe. Honestly, it has nothing at all to do with you."

I sat and I didn't say anything.

Kwame broke the silence. "But I still want to get to know you and I still wanna hang out with you and go out with you. I just want us to have an understanding that sex can't be an option. And hopefully soon you can start to see things the same way I do and look at your body as a temple of God, a temple that should be respected and a temple that reserves sex for marriage."

What the hell are you talking about? I wanted to ask. I almost started laughing in his face.

"So are you a virgin or something?" I asked while holding back smiles and laughter.

Kwame nodded, indicating that yes, he was in fact a virgin.

"Wow! So you like never had sex? Like never ever never? Never masturbated or nothing?"

Kwame shook his head no.

"Wow!"

A part of me looked at Kwame as a challenge and made me really want to fuck him that much more because he was a virgin, but another part of me couldn't have cared less about his religious convictions or his purity so long as he worked that out by his lonesome. Unfortunately, that latter side of me took over and I was ready to kick Kwame to the curb. I started my car back up and I headed in the direction of his apartment.

"Okay. I respect that. But I'm gonna drop you back off and I'm heading back to the party."

"Well, let me go back with you," he asked.

Nigga, you already wasted my time as it is and you damn sure ain't gonna be cramping my style anymore if you ain't giving up no dick.

That's what I wanted to tell him, but I was more cordial with him than that. I respectfully let him know that I wanted to go back to the party by myself.

When I dropped Kwame off at his place I told him that I would call him and that we would go out again. In my heart I knew that that probably wouldn't be the case. Kwame wasn't ready for me and I damn sure wasn't ready for his ass. I mean, he probably would have been good for me, but I had to be honest with myself. Where I was at, at that point in my life I knew that I had to live and do me and experience life to the fullest as a college student. And as far as I was concerned, I knew that my college experience was gonna include sex and a whole lot of it. So there was no sense in me tying myself down with a religious virgin during my freshman year. Nah, forget that, it was time for me to party and have fun.

I headed back to the Delta party and I immediately tracked down Kenya. I told her how the bug-a-boo had dissed me and didn't wanna fuck me.

Kenya was beyond shocked because she thought that I had already fucked Kwame and had him whipped. She told me to brush it off because there were bigger and better things that I had to attend to. Namely, she wanted me to meet the Q-dog who had been inquiring about me.

His name was LaMeek. He was one of the most popular Q's on campus. He was dark-skinned, muscular, about six feet four and he was also a star on the basketball team.

LaMeek was feeling me right off the bat and I was feeling him as well. Unlike with Kwame and his frontin' virgin ass, LaMeek was 'bout it 'bout it and he and I ended up fucking each other that night and many other nights that followed.

Fortunately for me, Kwame had remained persistent. He hung around and never gave up courting me or chasing me. Although it would take four years before I would end up calming down and getting complete control of myself and giving Kwame a shot at being my man, he would later prove to be a stabilizing force in my life.

Chapter Twenty-seven

D.E. Shaw & Co.

By the summer of 1996 I had graduated from college and I had decided to stay in D.C. and work full-time for the same brokerage firm that Andrea had originally hooked me up with years ago. The name of the brokerage firm was D.E. Shaw & Co. and they had offices in New York, D.C., and a few other cities. I was hired as a financial analyst with a starting salary of 60,000 dollars a year for a job that I absolutely loved.

Prior to graduating from Howard University I had been working at D.E. Shaw & Co. during all of my breaks from school. In 1994 when I was a junior and had gotten my second installment of 250,000 dollars from my mother's life insurance policy, I had decided that I wasn't gonna blow it like I'd done with the first installment of money. I talked to my boss and I asked him for some financial advice on what I should do with the money. My boss told me about a guy named Jeffrey Bezos who was working with D.E. Shaw & Co. and how he was leaving to start a company of his own called Amazon.com. If he was me he would take 200,000 dollars of the money and invest it in Amazon.com before the company went public and was listed on the stock market. With the other 50,000 dollars he told me to just play it and keep it in a money market fund.

At the time I didn't really know much of the intricate details about finance and investing but I decided to listen to my boss. He worked it out where for my 200,000 dollars I was able to buy 200,000 private shares of Amazon.com.

"Just wait and in a few years when Amazon. com goes public you'll be able to cash in on your investment," my boss said. "That's where I'm putting a large chunk of my money and I wouldn't tell you to do something that I wasn't also willing to do myself."

Although I didn't fully understand what I was investing in at the time, I trusted my boss and went with his advice. I never thought too much about the money after that point. All I knew was that it had been invested by people who were much smarter than I was, which was definitely a better alternative than blowing it on bottles of champagne at the club.

I had told Andrea what I had decided to do with the money and she thought that I was making a good move. If I couldn't see and have access to the money she reasoned, it would be less of a temptation for me to touch it and blow it and I would be less inclined to splurge with it and get myself into all kinds of trouble.

Well, by 1997 the whole world had gone dotcom crazy and by that time I had gained real-life practical experience as a financial analyst. I fully knew what I was holding in terms of that 200,000 dollar investment that I had made in Amazon.com. All I could say is that I basically had been fortunate enough and blessed enough to have been in the right damn place at the right damn time! Never in my wildest dreams did I ever think that I would be so fortunate to experience what was about to happen me.

What was about to happen was that on May 15, 1997 Amazon.com was scheduled to go public on the NASDAQ stock exchange at a price of eighteen dollars a share. With me holding 200,000 shares it meant that I was gonna instantly become a multimillionaire! By simply multiplying my 200,000 shares by the eighteen-dollar a share stock price, it meant that the shares in Amazon.com that I was holding were gonna be worth 3.6 million dollars and that my net worth would increase by 200,000 dollars every time the stock price increased by one dollar!

I had spoken to Andrea just about every day during that week leading up to Amazon.com going public and she was absolutely shocked by the whole Amazon thing.

"Baby, you see, this is not by accident, your meeting me was no accident, my helping you get that job at D.E. Shaw was no accident, you blowing that first installment of money was no accident, and Shayla, if this isn't confirmation from God that *everything* that you ever went through in your life has happened for a reason then I don't know what it is," Andrea said to me.

I knew that Andrea was right and I listened to everything that she was telling me. The thing that I respected the most from Andrea was that here she was listening to me telling her how I was about to come into all of this money and not once did she ever ask me for a dime; not even in a joking way did she insinuate that she wanted me to hit her off with some money. In fact, when I would tell her that I was gonna do this and do that for her or give her money, she didn't wanna hear it and she insisted that there was no way that she could ever let me do that.

"Shayla, when you get that money the only thing that I want you to do is to pray and ask God for guidance on how to best use that money and trust me, He'll direct you because He's blessing you like this for a reason."

Kwame and I had been becoming more and more of committed item with each passing day. He was still very religious and into the church. I was slowly coming along and getting into God, but at my own pace. What I liked and respected about Kwame was that he never spiritually mugged me and forced his views and beliefs on me so that they would align with his. He always just accepted me for who I was and where I was in my life while letting me experience God and religion on my own terms. Like Andrea, Kwame was elated for me and what was going to be my newfound wealth, but he too insisted that that was to be my money and that he wouldn't feel right taking anything from me.

I couldn't believe it because for all of my life I had been used to people using me and abusing me and exploiting me to their advantage. Now here I was with Kwame and Andrea proving to be two of the most loyal and genuine people in the world and they didn't want a thing from me other than my happiness. The way things were playing themselves out, I just knew that it had to be God. It just had to be.

Well, May, 15, 1997 had finally arrived and Amazon.com did in fact go public at eighteen dollars a share. I didn't sell my shares right away because there was so much demand for the stock. I held on to my shares for another four months until the stock price reached fifty-four dollars. At that point I sold off nine million dollars' worth of shares and I still had 1.8 million dollars' worth of the stock left in my brokerage account! It was the best present that I could have given myself for my twenty-fourth birthday.

Just like that, almost overnight it seemed, me, the promiscuous girl who had experienced more than my fair share of heartaches was sitting on top of the world and also sitting on a pile of nine million dollars in cash!

It was unbelievable.

Chapter Twenty-eight

The Truth Shall Set You Free—Late Summer 2002

Kwame and I had been married for four years. My life of promiscuity was something that was now way in my past. I was a Christian woman and fully devoted to God. Despite the fact that I had basically given up all hope of having a healthy relationship with my father, who had chosen to skip my wedding, I can honestly say that those four years of marriage had been the best four years of my entire life. Kwame had become a full-time minister at the AME church that he and I attended in Alexandria, Virginia where we lived. When I wasn't volunteering at the church-owned day care center I basically stayed home, lived lavishly, and spoiled myself in a healthy way. Since money wasn't an issue, Kwame and I, traveled and took trips and cruises all of the time and basically enjoyed each other, enjoyed life and what God had blessed us with.

Kwame showed me the way a real man was supposed to treat a woman. He treated me like royalty and he worshiped the ground that I walked on. I wanted nothing more than to have his children. I was also looking forward to raising a child and giving that child the life that I had wished and hoped for from the time I'd lost my mother at the age of five.

Unfortunately, with me looking forward to my twenty-ninth birthday, I didn't realized that I was about to get blindsided and walloped by two devastating turns of events.

The first thing was that I learned that my promiscuous lifestyle from years ago had finally caught up with me. To my complete lack of knowledge, I had contracted a sexually transmitted disease known as HPV (human papillomavirus), which had never manifested with any visible symptoms but which ultimately led to me getting cervical cancer.

Yes, cervical cancer, which meant that I would never be able to have kids and even more drastic, it meant that I could possibly lose my life.

That was the first major blow that sent me reeling into depression. But I couldn't stay depressed and sulking and feeling sorry for myself for too long because shortly thereafter, I found out more shocking news.

With the advance in DNA technology—technology that wasn't available at the time that Antonio Reid was on trial, he was able to request what is known as a post-conviction DNA test. Even though it had been close to eleven years from the time that I had been raped and ten years from the date that Antonio Reid had been convicted, the post conviction DNA test was able to prove with a 99.9 percent rate of accuracy that Antonio Reid was *not* the person responsible for raping me.

Based on the results of the post-conviction DNA test, Antonio Reid's lawyers and the Manhattan district attorney's office, where Andrea had since retired from, filed a motion to immediately vacate his conviction. After ten years of being in prison for a crime that he didn't commit, Antonio Reid was able to walk out of prison a free man.

"Why me?" That's all I could say to Andrea and Kwame. "Why me?"

Why did I have to be the victim of such devastating news? Why was God, who had delivered me from so much, allowing me to now go through what I was going through?

"Baby, you can't question God," my husband said to me.

"Kwame, don't give me that shit! You and Andrea both had been preaching to me about how God had put me through what I had gone through for a reason and that He was blessing me because of all that I had been through. So is this so-called God schizophrenic, does He have a split personality or what? How do you explain this bullshit?" I vented.

Andrea and Kwame both sat quiet and they let me vent.

"And Andrea, what do I say to a man whose life I ruined? The man spent ten years of his life in jail for something he didn't even fucking do? Oh, God, I feel like shit! How can he get those years back?" I said as I started breaking down and crying.

Andrea and my husband both didn't have any words for me and what could they really say? What do you say to someone who has just found out that they have cancer and who also just found out that they were solely responsible for ruining an innocent man's life?

"Kwame, please call my father and talk to him and let him know in so many ways that if he even thinks about calling here that I will get in my truck and drive down to New York and kill his sorry fucking ass!" I screamed. I meant every word that I had said. With Antonio Reid's reversal of conviction getting so much news coverage I was sure that my father would be calling me just to put salt on my wounds and pump himself up with his own sick form and sick sense of reverse vindication.

"Shayla, the first thing that you need to do is stop cursing like you're doing," Kwame said.

"Kwame, don't tell me that. I'm not trying to hear it. What the hell am I supposed to do?" I asked.

"You're supposed to trust God no matter what?" Kwame calmly said.

"Shayla, God works everything out for the good of those that love Him," Andrea added.

I sucked my teeth and I didn't say anything else. Then Andrea reminded me that her office was the one who had prosecuted Antonio Reid and that she probably was feeling just as bad as I was.

"And you know what? I'm not gonna sit around here and watch you sulk and throw a pity party, Shayla. What we're both gonna do is take our asses back to New York, look Antonio Reid and his family right in the eyes and apologize from the bottom of our hearts for what we in essence put him through. And Shayla, at the end of the day, what else can we do?"

I sat on my living room sofa in my plush 750,000 dollar home and I just was numb. I couldn't believe that my past still had such a hold on me, but apparently that hold was very strong and it didn't want to let go.

As the day went on and progressed, I knew that no matter what I just couldn't let myself slip back into that mental prison that I had been trapped in for such a big part of my life. All I could do was face the truth and tell the truth, and the truth was the only thing that could really set me free.

Facing that truth meant admitting that, yes, I had engaged in risky behavior in my past and that was what led to me getting cervical cancer. I would have to deal with that present reality by facing up to it in the present and not by living in the past. As far as Antonio Reid was concerned, I had to face him and tell him the truth, and the truth was that I had sincerely thought that he was indeed the man who had raped me.

Now, as it turned out, I was sincerely wrong and I couldn't stay stuck in that mistake that I had made. The only way I wasn't gonna stay stuck was by confronting Antonio Reid and allowing myself to admit and face the truth in the present and not run from the past.

Chapter Twenty-nine

Real Power

On the last Monday in September 2002, Andrea, Kwame and myself boarded a plane and we headed to New York. We were planning to meet Antonio Reid and some of his family members at his mother's home, which was located in Roosevelt, Long Island.

For the entire duration of the trip my palms were sweaty. I was beyond nervous, and at a complete loss of words in terms of what I was going to say to Antonio Reid. I have to admit that I was also a little apprehensive as to what his reaction would be to me when he was to eventually see me. Like, I didn't know if he was gonna just rush me and try to beat the crap outta me or what. If he did, I can't say that I wouldn't blame him for it.

Well anyway, after our plane landed and we had rented a car, we made the twenty-five minute ride out to Roosevelt. We eventually pulled in front of a very dilapidated one-story cape-style house. The grass in the front yard was full of dirt patches and crabgrass and there was a sick-looking pregnant dog that was running loose behind the white picket fence that was falling apart.

Kwame, Andrea, and myself made our way to the front door of the house and after being sniffed by the pregnant dog, we rang the front bell. The door was opened by a young girl who looked to be no older than four years old.

"Hello sweetie, is Antonio home?" Andrea asked.

The little girl didn't answer. She ran off, yelling to her grandmother that some people were at the front door.

Before long the little girl's grandmother came to the door and she cordially asked us to come in. She explained that they had been waiting for us to come. She invited us to sit down in the living room and she asked us if we wanted anything to eat or drink but we respectfully declined.

"Antonio," she yelled. "The prosecutor and the young lady and a gentleman are here to see you."

We waited in silence for about two minutes for Antonio to arrive. During that time the young girl who had opened the door for us came up to me and began showing me her baby dolls and trying to get me to play with her. She was the cutest thing and she was full of such innocence.

Finally Antonio appeared from one of the rooms that were situated toward the back of the house. He was dressed in jeans and sneakers and he also had on a Sean John T-shirt. He no longer had that scruffy beard and what was surprising was that he actually looked healthier and younger and more fit than he had looked when he was on trial.

The three of us stood up to greet Antonio and my heart was beating and my palms were still sweaty.

"No, sit, relax," he said as he sat down in a chair across from us.

There was a moment of awkward silence and then both Antonio and I tried to speak at the same time. He then gestured for me to speak first.

"Mr. Reid," I said as I shook my head and began to tear up, "I just wanna say from the bottom of my heart, that I am so, so, so sorry for what I put you through. I know that words can't reverse time, and it can't reverse anything so my words may not do much to help anything but I just felt, as did Ms. Boswell, that it was important for me to come and personally apologize to you face-to-face."

Antonio nodded his head and acknowledged my apology. Then Andrea apologized and Antonio nodded to her and acknowledged her apology.

I was sort of bracing and I was waiting for him to give us this fierce tongue lashing but surprisingly he didn't give us a tongue-lashing. Instead he did begin to talk to us in a very low, deliberate and reserved manner.

"You see that lady sitting right there?" Antonio asked us as he pointed to his mother.

We looked at her and nodded our heads.

"That's my mom. She is the *only* one who rode with me and stood by me and in my corner for the duration of my time. My friends bailed out on me. My relatives bailed out on me. My kids bailed out on me. What hurt me the most was when my fiancée bailed out on me and told me that she couldn't do the time with me and ended up getting married to someone else." He paused and tears began to well up in his eyes.

"If my girl could have just rode it out with me it would have been easier for me to deal with the time and do the time. But her, and everybody else who supported me so strong in the beginning, after like two years they all started dwindling down that support and a lot of them even started doubting whether or not I was truly innocent. I can't begin to tell you how much that hurt me."

I couldn't help but break down and cry. All I could do was repeatedly apologize to him.

"Shayla, it's all right," Antonio said to me. "I told you that that woman over there, my mother, she got me through this. It was her wisdom and her strength that I was leaning on, and if she wasn't there for me I wouldn't have made it through this. I mean, look around this room, you can see that we don't have much and that I don't come from much. But the one thing that my mother could give me was the ability to have faith and my faith was the thing that helped get me through this ordeal."

I nodded and looked at Antonio and I couldn't believe that he wasn't coming across as angry, bitter, or upset.

"See, after like my seventh year in prison, my mother told me and taught me that I had to learn to forgive and just let go. She told me that until I learned to do that and learned to come to peace with that, that I wouldn't be able to excrcise any power over my situation," Antonio explained. While he was talking his mother spoke up and elaborated on what he was saying.

"There's things that we're all gonna go through in our lives and not understand why we're going through what we are going through. We'll be unjustly accused of things that we didn't do, we'll be victims of senseless things that are unjust and unfair, and in those circumstances we'll feel so powerless and like victims and we'll want justice, and in most circumstances we'll be deserving of justice. But the thing that the Lord has taught me over the years is that the power that we all have and what no one can take away from us is our ability to forgive and let go of indiscretions that are perpetrated upon us. See, there is power in the ability to forgive, but you have to choose to exercise that power and when you do you will be at total peace with the circumstances that you cannot control."

When she was done talking, Antonio spoke up. He said to me that he had forgiven me years ago and that he had decided to let his anger and bitterness and resentment go because he knew he was innocent and that was the peace that he let resonate in his soul.

"Wow," I said in a low tone. It was like I just couldn't believe what I was hearing.

"Shayla, there is one thing that I do wanna know. I guess it's something that I always wanted to know. And that is, did you honestly in your heart of hearts think that I was the man who had raped you?" Antonio asked me.

Before speaking, I looked Antonio square in the eyes and I slowly nodded and I said, "Antonio, I honestly believed that it was you. There's no way that I would have accused you if I didn't," after I said that, I broke down again and started crying.

"You know what, I believe you, and that just confirms the decision that I had made long ago to forgive you," Antonio said.

My husband spoke up and he asked Antonio if there was anything that he and I could personally do to help right the wrong that was committed against him.

"Well, just pray for me, that's all," he responded.

I could absolutely not believe Antonio's humility. I was about to speak up and then he started speaking again. "See, listen, I can keep it real. I mean, there's obviously things that I wish would have turned out differently. I wish I hadn't lost that relationship with my children and my fiancée and all of those years in general, but that's in the past and I have to just move on. I don't want anything from you all because all that will do is keep me locked in the past and I've moved on from there. I'm at peace and I'll be fine. But if you wanna do something for me then just do it for my kids and that would be more than anything that I could ever ask."

I immediately reached inside my pocketbook for a pen and I asked Antonio for the names of his children and I wrote them down. Then I asked Antonio's mother for her name and she gave it to me and I wrote that down too. I then proceeded to write three separate checks in the amount of 500,000 dollars each and I handed them to Antonio. He looked shocked and he frowned his face up and then he looked at me.

"Is this real?" he asked me.

I nodded and told him that the checks were as good as gold.

"Oh no, I can't take this, then," he replied.

"That's why I didn't make those checks out to you. Those are checks for your children and their education or for whatever it is that they wanna do with the money. And Mrs. Reid, that other check is for you to do whatever it is that you wanna do. You can pay off your mortgage, you can buy a new home, you can go on a vacation or do whatever it is that you wanna do," I said.

Antonio and his mom both looked stunned. I could tell that they both felt very uncomfortable taking that kind of money from me. I just hoped in my heart that they would take the money and accept it as just a small gesture on my part to try and further make amends for the wrong that I had done and the error that I had made in having accused Antonio of rape.

***

Thankfully, Antonio and his mom did accept the money that I had put forth. What was so ironic was that I had come to New York to make a formal apology to Antonio and I was initially scared and apprehensive about how the outcome of the meeting would unfold. As it turned out all of my fears of meeting Antonio had been unwarranted. What ended up happening was that Antonio had basically helped to confirm the depth and trueness of something that my mom had told me when she had visited me in my dream and told me, *"And baby, if you don't remember anything else, just remember that you can and you will overcome anything that comes your way, but you're gonna have to first forgive and let go."*

On the entire plane ride back home I was a ball of snot and tears. I just couldn't stop thinking about how noble Antonio Reid's character was, and how he had moved me so much. As I sat in my window seat and looked at the beautiful clouds that the plane hovered over, I realized that God had used Antonio as a living sacrifice for me to learn firsthand the power of forgiveness.

If Antonio Reid was so willing to graciously forgive me for what I had done to him, then who in the hell was I to not forgive someone for the wrongs that had been perpetrated against me?

Right then and there I had made up my mind that I was going to do whatever I had to do in order to locate my nanny from back in the days, Joyce, and let her know that I forgave her for what she had introduced me to and had done to me. I was also gonna forgive Earl for what he had done to me, and I was gonna forgive my father for the way that he raised me and spoke to me and viewed me, and I was gonna make sure that from the bottom of my heart I forgave my mom for having passed away when I was so young. But most importantly, I was going to truly forgive myself for all of the bad decisions that I had ever made in my life and let the baggage go once and for all.

Yup, on that plane ride I was having an epiphany of just how and why I needed to exercise *real power*. With that epiphany I was truly freed from that mental prison that I had been in for close to twenty years, because finally I would be able to truly forgive myself and everyone else who had contributed to my life as a promiscuous girl.

On the programs that were handed out at my mother's funeral years ago, was a scripture from

Romans 8:28 and it read: And we know that all things work together for good to those who love God.

I had never understood just exactly what that scripture meant because I never could see or understand how all things, particularly bad things like car accidents, or rapes, or murders could work together for good. But as I sat on that plane it finally all became crystal clear that when God is in control that even what the devil meant for bad God could somehow turn it around and use it for good.

Epilogue

With the help and unconditional support of her husband Kwame, Shayla went on to beat her battle with cervical cancer and although she was never able to bear any children of her own, through her nonprofit organization that she started for at-risks youth, she was affectionately referred to as "mom" by many of the young men and women who had come through her organization seeking help. She had a huge, positive impact on the lives of thousands of young men and women who had been victims of molestation, incest, and rape. In running her nonprofit organization she realized that everything that had ever happened to her had finally come full circle. There was nothing that gave her more joy than positively impacting exploited, abused, and scarred young men and women.

Shayla and Andrea continued to be lifelong friends and she continued to refer to Andrea as her mom.

Shayla was able to personally confront Joyce, Earl, and her father and let them know that she forgave them. Although all three of them had become very defensive and even attacked her character, she felt good about the interaction that she had had with them, simply because she was resolute about who *really* had the power.

The statute of limitations for rape victims in the State of New York is only five years, which meant that even if Shayla's true rapists had been caught they would not have been able to be indicted and convicted for the crime, but as far as Shayla was concerned, it was okay, because the rapists didn't yield any more power over her simply because she had forgiven the true rapists and she was able to move on with her life.

ORDER FORM
URBAN BOOKS, LLC
78 E. Industry Ct
Deer Park, NY 11729

Name: (please print):_____

Address:_____

City/State:_____

Zip:_____

QTY	TITLES	PRICE
	16 On The Block	$14.95
	A Girl From Flint	$14.95
	A Pimp's Life	$14.95
	Baltimore Chronicles	$14.95
	Baltimore Chronicles 2	$14.95
	Betrayal	$14.95
	Black Diamond	$14.95

Shipping and handling-add $3.50 for 1st book, then $1.75 for each additional book.
Please send a check payable to:
Urban Books, LLC
Please allow 4-6 weeks for delivery

ORDER FORM
URBAN BOOKS, LLC
78 E. Industry Ct
Deer Park, NY 11729

Name: (please print):_____

Address:_____

City/State:_____

Zip:_____

QTY	TITLES	PRICE
	Black Diamond 2	$14.95
	Black Friday	$14.95
	Both Sides Of The Fence	$14.95
	Both Sides Of The Fence 2	$14.95
	California Connection	$14.95
	California Connection 2	$14.95

Shipping and handling-add $3.50 for 1st book, then $1.75 for each additional book. Please send a check payable to:

Urban Books, LLC

Please allow 4-6 weeks for delivery